lesley howarth says:

Carwash

Loony Luke's Carwash. The card that came through the door was irresistible. I have a confession to make — and an apology. When Luke came round to wash my car a couple of summers ago, I couldn't resist asking him if I could use the name of his business for a story. I ended up putting this conversation into *Carwash*!

The relationship between real life, the things that inspire a story, and the story itself, is a complicated thing to explain. The most honest thing I can say is that the 'story' Luke is not the real Luke; 'Middlehill' is not the village I live in, although it is loosely similar in layout. Characters are invented, settings rearranged. As in a dream, they take their existence from the imagination, which can transform the smallest thing into something that has a life of its own — one of the things that Liv learns during the course of *Carwash*. Liv's experiences are loosely based around those of an old school friend of mine; Lakey Park is a place we used to go to; the jar buried on the island is a jar that we really buried.

But this is giving away too many secrets, and there's someone at the door. Someone in a yellow mac — would I like my car washed?

Some other books by Lesley Howarth

I MANAGED A MONSTER
ULTRAVIOLET

Lesley Howarth lives in Cornwall and is the author of *Maphead*, winner of the Guardian Children's Fiction Award, and *Weather Eye*, which won the Smarties Prize.

lesley howarth

CARWASH

PUFFIN BOOKS

For Mary, wherever she is

PUFFIN BOOKS

Published by the Penguin Group
Penguin Books Ltd, 80 Strand, London WC2R 0RL, England
Penguin Putnam Inc., 375 Hudson Street, New York, New York 10014, USA
Penguin Books Australia Ltd, 250 Camberwell Road, Camberwell, Victoria 3124, Australia
Penguin Books Canada Ltd, 10 Alcorn Avenue, Toronto, Ontario, Canada M4V 3B2
Penguin Books India (P) Ltd, 11 Community Centre, Panchsheel Park, New Delhi — 110 017, India
Penguin Books (NZ) Ltd, Cnr Rosedale and Airborne Roads, Albany, Auckland, New Zealand
Penguin Books (South Africa) (Pty) Ltd, 24 Sturdee Avenue, Rosebank 2196, South Africa

Penguin Books Ltd, Registered Offices: 80 Strand, London WC2R 0RL, England

www.penguin.com

First published 2002
1

Set in 12/16pt Monotype Joanna
Typeset by Rowland Phototypesetting Ltd, Bury St Edmunds, Suffolk
Made and printed in England by Clays Ltd, St Ives plc

British Library Cataloguing in Publication Data
A CIP catalogue record for this book is available from the British Library

ISBN 0-141-31079-0

Chapter 1

I've been calling myself Loony Luke for a while now, because of my Mad Summer Offers. When I started up the carwashing business again, I thought about Crazy Couch, or Mad Mark – my middle name – or Manic Wash 'n' Wax, but Dad said stick with 'Loony Luke's Carwash', and he couldn't of been more right. The number of cars in the village has doubled in the last couple of years, so any car-washing business was always going to be gold. My brother Danny told me I must be having a laugh when I started up the business the first time. Now he wishes he'd thought of it – good thing for him that 'Daggy Danny's Carwash' doesn't sound too clever!

Our house is a big old farmhouse, and it came with a massive field. That's the reason Dad bought the quad bike, to run round the field and round up the chickens. Danny wanted chickens. He swore he'd look after them. After he stood on one of them, and one drowned in its drinking water, and three flew off and got lost, he learned how to clip their wings. Then he goes, 'No more animals. Animals are a pain.'

Getting up on Sundays to wash cars is a pain, but Danny wakes me up anyway. This morning he's first on the quad before I get past the cats and chickens – his job to feed 'em, not mine.

'You never fed the chickens!' I let the whole village know. 'You deaf, or what – I said CHICKENS!'

He gives me the finger and almost rolls the quad, only just recovers and clips the tree by the fence.

'Hey, Danny, don't mind the tree!'

He legs it round the barn and covers me with mud, then guns it down the field. As he comes up again, I jump him. 'My turn.'

He tries to pass. 'You wish.'

'I'll tell Dad about the circular saw.'

He revs round me, round the barn, and away down the field again. Next circuit, I give it to him straight. 'Cir-cu-lar saw, CIR-CU-LAR SAW!'

'Shut it, will you?' That brings him in.

'Get off then.'

'I'm *getting* off.' Danny brings in the 'Firestarter', a brand-new 50cc All-Terrain quad bike, sports styling, automatic gears, adjustable throttle restrictor, fully adjusted to *Max*.

'Get off it, I said.'

'I *am*.' Just as I get my hand on the throttle, he revs away again.

'You almost took my arm off, you idiot!'

He gives me his vees with one hand.

'Mind the mud!' No prizes for guessing what happens next. 'I said, *mind the mud! Danny!*'

And he's bogged it already in that muddy place under the goalpost. I'm racing down the field like a madman, before he digs it in. 'Told you not go in there!'

'Didn't see it!' he says.

I wonder about him, sometimes. 'What, you didn't see the *goalpost?*'

'Didn't notice it,' he says.

Disaster-man guns the throttle. The wheels spin round in the mud. Now I have to dig him out of a mess, just like I do every day. Give Danny a stereo, knobs fall off it. A jar to unscrew, he'll break it. A disaster waiting to happen, that's what Danny is. He overdoes everything, I swear. Dad says, No feel for mechanical things. Watch him on the quad, Luke, Dad goes – like *I* can watch Danny on anything.

The wheels scream round in the mud. Now there's smoke coming out.

'Throttle back, you prat!' I reach him and grab the bike. 'Get round the back and push!' He pushes. I get on and give it some juice, and the wheels splatter Dan with mud from head to foot, so he looks like a yeti or something.

'Oh, *yuk!*' he goes, jumping around like someone scalded his foot.

I give him a final coating of mud, and take off, cruising once or twice round the field to show him how it's done. *And on his second circuit this promising newcomer takes the tyres wide . . .*

I take the quad through the tyres by the fence, over the hump by the pine tree, back wide of the goalposts, where mud-man's trying to find his eyes, through the tyres again, the sun just rising over the sewage farm now, flashing on our long landing window with the red and blue glass round the edges. The bathroom light pops on as Dad gets up. He's usually up before now. Guess the quad woke him up.

I'm caning the quad over the bank at the end of the field and burning down the other side of it by the old toilet covered in ivy, the engine roaring now, when suddenly I almost roll it coming over this concrete step covered in brambles.

Dad runs out of the house with a toothbrush in his mouth. 'Luke?'

'Yeah?'

'All right?'

'Forgot the step was there.'

'Mind what you're doing.'

'I am.'

'You almost rolled it.'

'No way.'

Close, all the same. Dan knows it. Dad's paranoid about rolling the quad. He must have spotted me from the bath-room. 'Stay away from those brambles,' he goes, 'and mind the bank at the end. Danny, that goes for you too.'

Quads can roll and crush you. You could trip up and fall down a hole. Choke on a burger. Fall down the stairs. You could accidentally lock yourself in the cruddy old bog at the bottom of the garden, and no one would find you until you'd turned into a skeleton or something. Quads are no more dangerous than going to school on the school bus, I told Mum when it arrived. I could see she was worried. Don't ride over rough ground, will you? she goes. I'm looking at her. Mum, it's an All-Terrain Vehicle. That's what ATV's are for.

Dad goes, Mind that paintwork. But quads are *meant* to be scratched. Farmers use them to round up their sheep. Quads are working bikes. Dad keeps an immaculate VW beetle in the barn. He shouldn't off-road at all. He can't get his head round the damage. Dad goes mad if you break anything. Danny breaks things all the time.

I can feel Dad watching me as I ride the quad up the field. When I turn, I can see him waving. I knew he'd flag me down.

I ride up and throttle back. 'What?'

'That'll do for now,' Dad says.

'But we only just came out here.'

'Haven't you got a job to do?'

'What job?'

'The carwash?'

'I'm doing it later, all right? It's not like I've forgotten.'

But Dad thinks he can run the business. 'Sunday morning. Too early for the quad. Better get ready now.'

'Nothing to get ready.'

'Luke.' He waits until I get off the bike. Then he goes in to clean his teeth.

I jump on and do a couple more circuits to let him know who's boss. Then I stable the quad. Danny follows me into the barn and breaks the tap while I'm getting out my buckets and bottles.

'Nice one – what did you do to it?' The tap spins round, but nothing happens.

'It was like that when I touched it,' Danny says. 'I never did anything to it.'

'You must have – why are you wet?'

'It wouldn't stop, so I turned and turned it –'

'Now you've rubbished the washer.'

'I told you, it was broken.'

'It is now. Leave the light switch alone.'

He's only flicked it a million times so it won't go on again. No feel for things, Dad says – Daniel Clinton Couch, the only man to foul up a tin-opener on a ring-pull can, because he didn't notice the ring-pull.

So I'm slugging cheap car shampoo into my bucket, adding some Premium Turtle Wax as well, good gear you're meant to use dry, but I bung it in with the washing water and it dries like a diamond, looks like you polished for hours – trade secret that – when I realize I need hot water.

'I'm going in for some hot water to melt in the Turtle Wax,' I'm telling Danno. 'How do I top up with cold, now you broke the outside tap?'

'Top up inside,' Dan sweats.

'Mum goes mad if I slop on the floor.'

'So what,' Dan goes. 'You won't.'

'You won't, you mean. Take this bucket.'

He looks at me.

'Go on,' I'm telling him, 'take it. I'll tell Dad you broke the tap.'

He takes the bucket.

'And this one.' I hold it out. 'Three-quarters hot, quarter cold, all right?'

He comes out with suds down his shorts. 'It was broken when I touched it,' he says.

'What was?'

'The tap in the barn.'

'Give me the buckets. Fill up the quad, all right?'

'You fill up the quad,' Dan goes.

'Circular saw.'

'All right.'

The circular saw gives me Ultimate Power till Dad finds out Danny broke it. Weekends, Danny and me chop up firewood. Danny only goes and feeds the leg of a bed into the circular saw last Saturday. Sure enough, it gags on a castor. Now when you start it up it wobbles and smokes and the drive-belt acts really weird. It's only a matter of time before Dad uses the circular saw and Danny has to 'fess up, so I have to use the leverage while it lasts. Once Dad finds out what Danny did to it, there'll be the stuff about Tools and Trust and Having a Feel For These Things and Why Didn't You Tell Me Before and This Will Have To Be Paid For. Dad goes mad if you break anything. Danny breaks things all the time.

'Fill up the quad,' I'm telling Danny, again. 'And put it away properly, all right?'

'I got it out,' he goes. 'So you should put it away.'

'Like that's ever going to happen, while you're my slave.'

'I'm not your stupid slave.'

'Tap. Dad. Circular saw.'

'Anything else, your majesty?' Danny kicks in the barn door.

'That's right, break that, as well.'

Desperate Dan disappears into the back of the barn where the petrol cans are kept.

I can't stop winding up him, once I start. 'Dark, is it, now you broke the light?'

'I never broke it,' he says.

'Funny it won't come on then,' I'm saying. 'Petrol's under the bench.'

'I know,' Danny goes. 'Isn't it enough that you're making me do this, but you've got to watch me, as well?'

'Moo-dy.'

Danny chucks out a bucket. Probably time to go.

So I'm off up the road with my buckets to wash Mrs Oliff's Corsa. It's a small car, takes less than ten minutes, plus Mrs Oliff tips well. Feels good to be back in business. Last summer I made a killing once I got the garage concession. Old Mr Kramer at Spring Point Garage let me wash cars on his forecourt for ten per cent of my takings. Once I got up to speed, I could wash and rinse a Mondeo in the time it took most people to fuel up and pay at the desk. Business went ballistic by the end of the holidays, people were filling up specially at Spring Point to get my Wash 'n' Wax Offer. Pity I only thought of asking old Kramer about the garage concession towards the end of the summer.

This year I'm not missing out, so I'm cranking it up with jobs round the village, then, when the holidays start, that's me up the garage again, hoping old Kramer remembers me. Most people tend to remember me, specially Barry The Post Office, after I ripped off his wing mirror last year. Usually

I put in some welly and get a good tip. Customer care is the secret. Make people want you back. 'Nice one, Luke,' they say. 'Book you again for next week?' All it takes is some chat and a really nice shine on their bonnet.

The Come Back Factor is huge with me. That's why I go the extra distance. People notice it, if you do. I had a good thing going, last year, hard to keep it under wraps in the end, I'd have had to employ an assistant if the holidays hadn't ended and I had to go back to school. Dad goes, You wouldn't think a carwash would go so well. No, I'm going. You wouldn't. No one twigs how much I make. I don't let on. I'm not stupid.

Mrs Oliff lives next to the Chapel with her old, scabby cat and her husband who's ill upstairs, who you never see. That's why I wash their car. But just when I reach the Chapel, I drop my shammy – my 'leather' for polishing off – and it's then that I spot her.

Village idiot up the tree. Mad Sylvie Bickle next door. Bix, they call her, she sits in the tree in the hedge and watches everything. Nobody bothers about her. They even forget that she's there. Her sister Liv is cool. Everyone wants to go out with her. No one mentions dingbat Bix. Liv asks them what they mean, if they do. What do you mean? she goes. My sister can sit where she wants.

She isn't embarrassed at all. That's what makes her so cool. It would probably destroy anyone else. Anyone else up the bus stop with a sister who sits up a tree, their life would be hell, and I'd be in that. But no one messes with Liv.

Liv, she walks up the road, and her hair swings from side to side, and she wears these really cool clothes. Paxman would die for it. Beddoes and Innit drool if she even walks by, they should be so lucky, Liv's a Year Eleven. I say 'hullo' if I see her. I might say 'hi' next time.

Mad Sylvie Bickle has fair hair, not like Liv at all, so it's easy to think she's adopted at birth, from a different planet, or something. Like me and Danny. You'd never pick us as brothers.

She's been ill or something, supposedly. I go to pick up my shammy, and I can see her white legs in the branches. Mad as a cat. Sly as a hound. Watching, whenever you look. Well up on me and Danny.

Mad bat Bix, up the tree.

I think, I probably know, worse luck, she's been watching us all the time.

Chapter 2

They call me Bix. I sit up the tree. Most people think I'm mad.

I don't call myself a Loony to make people laugh and get business. Luke Couch, going down the road with his buckets, thinking he's so great. I shouldn't actually say it. But Luke Couch actually *does*.

I've seen how he is with Dan. I actually said to him once, Not very nice to him, are you? Who? he says. Three guesses, I said. I've seen how you push him around. Mind your own business, you freak, he says, going down the road with his hands on his head like he owns the village or something. His back says, Like it or lump it. Any complaints to Mr Popular.

Any added examples of Luke Couch bullying anyone, please post to Sylvie Bickle, The Ash Tree, Hedge Between Our House And Luke's. I'm right over Loony Luke's head as he swings up the road with his buckets, and Danny clears out the barn. I saw him shove Dan off the quad and leave him to do all the work.

Now he's outside the Chapel. He's dropped his shammy-leather in the road, the thing he polishes cars with. He's always on about 'shammying off' being the secret of a good wash and wax. I hear him talking with Mrs Williams when he cleans her car next door. He pours on the charm with the old folk, it's enough to make anyone –

I think he might actually have seen me. He bent down to pick up his shammy just then and he had a good squiz up the tree, nosy hound, and I had to pull up my legs.

So Luke Couch sees me, so what? I don't actually care what he thinks, even though it feels like, this morning, we're the only people awake.

Except for Tiggy Bigglelowe, the noisy dog over the road.

I'm straight up the tree most Sundays, after the dog over the road wakes me up. It's impossible to sleep in this village. I especially like the sound of the quad bike next door tearing round the field at the crack of dawn, or whenever Danny Couch feeds his chickens. I'm sure it's fun to ride, but it's not actually so great to wake up to.

Lots of people tell me I say 'actually' too much. Actually, Bicks, can you shut it, they say. I don't mind them calling me Bicks. I never felt like a Bickle. Now I sign myself Bix. I never actually felt like a Sylvia. The tree helps me feel who I am. I feel lost when I'm down on the ground. And I might as well be Bix up the tree, as lying in bed listening to the Bigglelowes' dog over the road: Owf! Owf! Owf! Thanks for that, Mrs Bigglelowe.

Mrs Bigglelowe stakes Tiggy out on a Sunday morning at nine. Basically he's an ex-guard dog. He strains on his tether when anyone walks by. He'd like to rip off their faces. People in villages three miles away can hear the noise he makes. If you can sleep through this, you need to visit a doctor. Or else you can climb the tree in the hedge, and feel nice and cool and early.

Once I'm higher than Tiggy, it sometimes shuts him up. Me and the Hound of the Baskervilles eye each other through the tree. Surprising what you can see, if you get up with Tiggy Bigglelowe.

Our ash tree hangs over the road and makes a screen in summer, and keeps out the rest of the village. With Tiggy barking through it, invisible through the leaves, and Couch's place next door doing quad and mower noises, the world sounds noisy beyond it. My sister and I used to climb the tree when we were younger, and hang out over the road. Mrs Bigglelowe used to nag us. 'You girls, you want to be careful – does your mother know you're up that tree?'

The ash is much larger now, and Liv starts her A Levels in September. You could say we've grown up with it. I'm Year Ten in September. That's if I go back to school. I only just started Year Nine when I came down with glandular fever. Now I have to *convalesce*, which means I get to be bored out of my mind, and I have to lie down a lot. Even little things tire me. Liv says Elizabeth Barrett Browning convalesced until Robert Browning ran off with her. She'd be the one to know, doing A Level English Lit.

Now the place where we used to play tea-parties with mortar is lumpy and overgrown. Concrete blocks from the time we built the house are completely covered with ivy.

The compost bin and the fence have actually been pulled over and buried underneath it. Funny how landscapes change. You can see it all, up the tree.

Once the fence was ugly and new. I can remember it all. You wouldn't guess our house is almost sixteen years old, actually as old as Liv. The ash was just a sapling in tea-party days. Now it's a tree big enough to have SWEB out every three years to trim back its branches where they touch the power lines. Still every summer it puts out its leaves and the wood-pigeons coo in the branches and drive Dad mad, boo-hooing to each other at four in the morning, but I don't mind the sound. I love it up here in the summer, up in the cool tree-top, where you can see over the whole village and trace the lanes by the wormy green lines of trees, all the way up to the Top Road.

Luke Couch is out in the road now, making a start on the Corsa.

His bucket and scrapers are in Mrs Oliff's drive. I can just about see her kitchen window, and the Startups' house next door. From the top of the tree I can see up the road as far as the bend at White Cottage in one direction, which is just about the middle of the village, and down the road as far as Vine Cottage – the end of the village – in the other. Some-times I take up a cushion and sit in a crook of the branches. I'm almost up with the power lines. The electric and tele-phone cables run through the top of the tree, and I wonder when I watch them, why don't the birds get a shock?

Dad says the tree poses a threat to the cables. If I ever see a cable brought down, I'm to let it alone and come in. Not dance around with it, waving it about? I usually say, in my tired voice. You *would* dance around if you touched it, Dad says. So one day the SWEB men will come, and the tree will have to come down. Till then, I'll sit in it, thank you.

His head's bobbing around by the Chapel now. Means he's rinsing off. The flood down the road means I'm right. Mrs Oliff knows Luke uses a biblical flood of water to wash off the smallest car, so she parks it outside the Chapel to let the runoff run off. The Chapel has pictures of young people enjoying themselves at Youth Club outside on its notice-board, all five of them playing skittles, and trying to look like more. No one known to man has ever set foot in the Chapel. Wouldn't catch me or Luke there, which is about *all* we have in common.

Loony Luke, he calls himself, and everyone actually goes for it and books him to wash their car? Everyone laughs at his card. That boy. Got to hand it to him. Enterprise, that's what they call it. Pity they never see him duffing up his brother, or teasing people at the bus stop. Give and take you could call it, but personally, here up the tree, I'd like Danny to give some back.

A hose whips into the drive, and I know he's finished the rinse.

I've watched him wash cars enough to know there're two kinds of carwash, the kind where the customer watches and the kind where they leave him to it. He'll be flashing his leather 'shammy' in a minute, polishing off for that Loony Luke shine, the secret of his success.

Mrs Williams thinks the sun shines out of Luke's smile.

15

'Oh, Luke,' she says, 'what a marvellous shine – how on earth do you do it?'

Mrs Williams lives just round the corner. I can easily hear what they say.

Luke holds up his leather. 'You need a shammy,' he says.

'Sham-*wah*,' says Mrs Williams. 'Skin of an antelope, don't you know.'

Luke looks blank. 'You what?'

'Chamois, a goat-shaped antelope inhabiting lofty mountain ranges. So *that's* your magic touch,' she says, tipping Luke loads of dosh.

Actually anyone can get the skin of a goat-shaped antelope inhabiting lofty mountain ranges and go out cleaning cars and buffing Mrs Williams's Honda Civic till she can see her face in it. There's nothing magic about it. I should probably do it myself.

Hear the drum of water on the side of a car? That'll be Luke deciding to drill out the muck in the wheels with a blast of the hose. He'll be blocking the end of the hose with his horrible bitten finger, squeezing the water into a jet, then not being able to resist pelting Michael Paxman's garden next door, in the hope he'll be somewhere outside. He'll be nailing a cat when he gets bored with that, then drilling those alloys with water.

I've seen him hose people in the street before, and not accidentally, either. He specializes in using up enough water for two African villages per car. An NVQ in hose-use is Luke's idea of skill, a close second to expertise with the sham-*wah*, like there's anything *to* cleaning cars. He'd kill for ten minutes with a power-hose, but who has a power-hose and hires Luke to wash their car? They'd have to be loony themselves.

Like me, sitting up a tree.

Mum doesn't get the tree. How much you see up here. How cool and aloof you feel. Liv gets the tree, being cold and alone and above things, between the earth and the sky, because she studies Romantic poets. Romantic poets would have got the tree. Liv's preparing for A Level Lit over the summer. She's got the reading list. She knows all about the Romantics. Liv sees how a bird's-eye view gives you Loony Luke's game in a nutshell. Knowledge is power. Who said that?

Almost finished now. A flick of the shammy and he's done. It's taken him all of ten minutes, not bad for a three-fifty carwash, or whatever he's charging these days. Loony Luke, the Best Carwasher in the West. *Back and Better Than Ever.* That's what his latest card says.

He might be better than ever. Don't take my word for it. Give him a ring. Reel out your hose. See if you like the shine. I'm not saying his card isn't right. He even postered the door of the Boys' Brigade hut – 'The Return of Loony Luke' – between the posters for 'Dangerous Dave's Disco' and 'Line Dancing at The White Horse From The Twenty-Seventh', and 'Dancing to Local Group "Frenzy", the ninth and seventeenth of August'.

He does a good job, so they say. Everyone likes Loony Luke. But just you be a bit different in a way that isn't so funny. Get up a tree. Above yourself. Have opinions and use long words. Who does she think she is, they'll say, though I *am* actually above everyone else in the tree, and I can actually look down on them all.

Perhaps people who think people who don't think the same as them, think they're better than everyone else, would actually like to tell me how I can be above *myself*? Luke can get away with anything. If he said he had two brains, they'd laugh and say, 'What a character. That boy.' Luke can get away with being different, just for a joke.

But Luke's on a level with everyone. You can rely on Luke.

Chapter 3

'That cat again!'

Michael Paxman's father notices the largish black-and-white cat sitting on the wall dividing the back of the garden from Mrs Oliff's garden with annoyance. After a while it climbs stiffly down, as if it were eighty years old. In fact, the Bickles's cat is only five. Around its white bib it wears a reflective collar with a bell and a screw-topped cylinder, in which a tight roll of paper announces its name as 'Hodge'. The rest of the message – 'I choose to live with: Olivia Bickle, "Roseleigh", Middlehill, Alfington' – can only be made out with difficulty.

Hodge likes to pad over the crossroads from his home at the Bickles's house to Michael Paxman's garden at least once a day, very slowly. Dipping through the hedge at Mrs Oliff's, he pads up the Paxmans' drive, looking deceptively slow and old, narrowing in on the bird table, which is the apple of Mr Paxman's eye. There he sleeps in the grass, looking as though nothing will bother him. Many are the birds that are snared in this way, Hodge suddenly leaping up over the overhang of the bird table, taking down a wood-pigeon with a squawk and a flurry of feathers.

The Paxmans' garden, home of many birds, and a popular place for cool cats, lies behind the Chapel, not cool or popular at all, unless you happened to be a member of the sad-jumpered Youth Group.

Which Michael Paxman is.

Inside his house, The Orchard, coffee is brewing for Sunday morning elevenses. Michael Paxman's parents, both of them in their mid-fifties and old by comparison with the parents of his friends, will accompany it with digestive biscuits. A knotty quadratic equation lies unsolved on the kitchen table, Michael's hair mixing with his father's as they puzzle over his homework. It never occurs to either of them that they might not be able to crack it. Michael has been brought up to have an enquiring mind. His parents' interest in birds has seeped into Michael's personality without his really noticing it. He can't remember a time when he didn't know what a dunnock looked like. He knows a nuthatch too. Not many birds pass Michael Paxman by without his being able to identify them and produce their Latin names too, which puts him firmly into the category of genus Geekus Maximus himself, and gives him a dangerous secret. Should this knowledge leak out on the school bus to provide a new topic for tormentors like Luke Couch, his life will be Livingus Hellus.

The battle of wits waged by Michael Paxman's father against Hodge the black-and-white cat, who loves birds in his own way, has recently kicked up a notch. As spring turned into summer, Hodge's hit-list included fledgeling sparrows, whose numbers have fallen off dramatically nationwide, perhaps due to air pollution, but more probably due to Hodge.

Michael Paxman's father has been unable to resist making a few cutting remarks about cats in general, and Hodge in particular, in passing the Bickles's garden, where that girl always sits up the tree.

'Cats, an ecological disaster,' he mumbles, in passing. 'A responsible cat owner would put a bell on its collar.'

'Hodge *has* got a bell,' the ash tree tells him sharply.

Mr Paxman looks up.

'A device firing random ping-pong balls,' he announces into the leaves above him, 'has so far failed to scare your cat. I have also tried a noxious-smelling chemical, but your cat still comes into our garden.'

Bix reports back.

'I'm sorry about our cat,' Mrs Bickle has responded to Michael Paxman. 'I should put the hose on him if he comes into your garden after birds.'

'Oh, I wouldn't like to do that,' says Michael Paxman.

'It'll teach him a lesson. Hodge is a wuss. Tell your dad it's worth a try.'

Michael Paxman reports back.

'The hose, eh? Right,' Mr Paxman decides. 'This is war.'

So far the hose has missed him. Whenever it narrowly passes him, Hodge only watches the water and wonders what it can be for.

But today is Hodge's unlucky day. His daily stroll across

the junction not only triggers Tiggy Bigglelowe into the usual tempest of barking, but coincides with Mrs Oliff's carwash and Luke's decision to pelt Michael Paxman's garden with the business end of the hose.

Hodge sits down under the bird table as a wavering finger of water piles out of the sky. Hodge flattens his ears very slightly as the arc of water falling from the sky boils flowers out of their flowerbeds, sets hanging baskets rocking, and pounds across the grass. He's seen this water before. It's nothing to worry about.

On the other side of the hedge, Luke tires of throttling the hose. *'Hey, Paxman, enjoy your shower!'* Unlikely Sad Man Paxman will be out in his garden anyway. *'Get that, Mr World at War, reading war magazines at the bus stop!'*

'What on earth is that?' Michael Paxman's father jumps up. A thudding jet of water crosses the conservatory roof.

Luke's parting shot with the hose flushes Mr Paxman and Michael out of the house in seconds, upsetting the quadratic equation that was just about to crack. The retreating finger of water faints over the grass. Hodge half-rises. Experience tells him that the water won't hit him. He holds his nerve until the last moment. As incredibly, *the water reaches him,* Hodge takes off like a bullet.

Michael tugs at his sweater.

'What's the matter with you?' his father says.

'Copped a neckful of water when I opened the conservatory door.'

'Someone messing about with a hose.' Mr Paxman searches the sky. 'Thank-you-very-much!'

'It's Luke Couch – of course.' Michael points next door. 'Washing Mrs Oliff's car.'

'Sorry about that.' Luke's bullet head appears over the wall. 'Hose went mad when I dropped it.'

'I should say it did,' says Michael Paxman's father, severely. 'Look what you've done to my bulbs.'

'I c'n plant 'em again,' Luke shrugs. 'Weed it for you, if you like.'

'I can weed it myself, thank you. Do you always drench the neighbours' gardens when you wash someone's car?'

'Only if they pay extra,' Luke jokes. He clears his throat. 'Have to give it some welly to get the muck under the splashline. Squeeze the end like this –' he demonstrates with the turned-off hose – 'it works like a power-hose.' He eyes the Paxmans' Rover, grey with farm-muck below the splashline. 'Loony Luke's Carwash – give you a card?'

'You're having a laugh,' Michael says.

But, incredibly, his father crosses the garden and takes the printed card that Luke hands over the hedge. *Cool Hand Luke. Best Carwasher in the West.* He taps it against his fingers. Reads the legend, smiles. 'Used to clean windows myself, when I was a lad.'

'Cheap summer rates coming up.'

'How about we don't charge you for ruining our garden,' says Michael, with spirit, 'and then you clean our car.'

'Two Cars Cleaned for the Price of One, not including valet, offer closes end of July,' Luke continues smoothly. 'Sorry about the hose. Hope I didn't scare the cat.'

'What cat?'

'One that streaked over the road.'

'You did me a favour actually,' Mr Paxman acknowledges.

'That Bickles's cat, eating your birds?'

'Has been, up until now.'

'Don't worry,' Luke says. 'I'll stop him.'

'I should think you've done enough,' Mr Paxman says, mildly.

'Leave it to me,' Luke says again, as though there's an understanding between them from which Michael Paxman's father will only withdraw with difficulty. 'I'll fix it.'

On their return to the kitchen, the coffee is cold. Mrs Paxman reheats it.

'Unusual boy.' Michael Paxman's father broods over Loony Luke's card, as the maths homework gives up its secrets.

'Dead unusual,' Michael says.

'Talk to him much on the bus?'

'Not a lot,' Michael says.

That evening, Mr Paxman takes a walk around the village. On his return, the shine of her newly Luked Corsa flags Mrs Oliff's house, a scarlet flash in the road.

A flurry of snarling at ear-level causes Mr Paxman to jump away from the raised edge of the Bigglelowes' lawn. That evil hound again. Good job it's tethered up.

'Nasty piece of work, wants castrating,' he notes aloud, still admiring Luke's handiwork. Eat your lunch off that car. Look at the finish on it. 'Loony Luke's Carwash', eh? Takes a pride in his work. Put his back into washing that vehicle. Not often you see a job well done, these days. A job well done these days is as rare as a . . . meadow pippit.

Mr Paxman turns into his drive.

'That lad's done a proper job on Joan Oliff's Corsa,' he tells Mrs Paxman, parking his hat.

'Which lad?' Michael frowns.

'Your friend Luke. You could take a leaf from that boy's book. Chat to people more.'

'You are joking,' Michael says.

'Puts himself out for people. Enterprising lad.'

'He's out to make money,' Michael snaps. 'Everyone thinks he's their friend.'

'You don't,' his mother says, perceptively for once. 'He seems a nice boy. Knows everyone. You should talk to him more. You might have something in common.'

Being alive at the same time is about the only thing that occurs.

'You don't know what he's like.'

'What *is* he like?' Michael's mother asks.

Michael Paxman's imagination falls down at the thought of describing Luke Couch. Three words should do it, but which three words?

'You don't want to know,' Michael says.

'I really think,' his father says, 'you should give people a chance and get to know them –'

Paxman jumps up in rage and frustration. If only they *knew*. Three words for Luke Couch? Insensitive. Annoying. Git.

For one thing, waiting for the school bus every morning has been made a misery for him for at least the last six months by Loony Luke's large and unpredictable personality, and the occasional focusing of it upon the boy who tries to read quietly. For another, Liv Bickle thinks he's stupid, the only person on the bus he particularly didn't want to look stupid in front of, since Luke quizzed him about chart bands within her hearing, which he knew that he, Michael, knew nothing about. Plus he has to hide the things he *does* know, and never let on that he's clever in class, as that would make the bus stop unbearable and he'd have to stop *going* to school.

Four, mad Sylvie Bickle has sussed the fact that he's different and never leaves him alone. Five, Nathan Beddoes alternately torments him and jokes with him, Michael, at the bus stop, so that alliances are always uncertain and his nerves are always on edge. Six, Chris Turpitz, called Innit, sits next to him and drives him mad because everything he says is *that* obvious, innit?

Seven, just about his only ally at the moment is Dan Couch, Loony Luke's brother, who will actually sometimes step in when Luke goes over the top, if you count a member of his own family as your best defence against Luke.

'He only apologized because *you* were there,' Michael Paxman says, feelingly.

'Who apologized, where?' Mr Paxman scans the papers.

'Luke Couch. Hosing the garden. He meant the hose for me.'

'An accident, I should think,' Mrs Paxman murmurs,

filling in an order form for a Limited Edition china plate entitled 'His Last Walk', showing a sad collie needing a bandage removed from its leg. 'He wouldn't go annoying folk. He probably needs the business.'

'Thinks he can get away with anything because of his stupid carwash.'

'Programme on tonight about the Origins of Life.' Michael Paxman's father scouts the television schedules. 'Or are you going to Youth Club?'

'Don't know,' Paxman mumbles.

'Speak clearly, please, Michael.'

'I'm not sure yet.' Paxman raises his voice. 'The options are too exciting.'

'No need to be sarcastic, Michael,' his father says. 'Did that curry at tea-time upset you?'

Over the Chapel a summer night falls as Paxman stamps up to his room to change his damp jumper for a sadder version of the one Luke soaked with the runoff from his last blast with the hose on the Paxman's conservatory roof, as outside and round the village rings the sound of Tiggy Bigglelowe, barking away the hours.

Chapter 4

Confessions of Bix, Part Two. Our cat streaked in the other day, soaking wet. It actually wasn't even raining. Maybe he fell in Paxmans' pond? Hodge leads a double life. I know Mrs Oliff feeds him. Then he comes home and eats more.

Our last cat was called Alfie. He was hit by a car in Raggin Lane when he was six months old. Tractors pound up that lane and Keith Hurst Kevs down it in his black Nova with the sound system pumping, and an exhaust you can hear in three counties. He's not about to notice a Please Drive Carefully Through the Village sign, let alone a smallish black cat.

We never found out what hit him. Eventually we found Alfie dead under a bush in a garden off Raggin Lane. He was stiff and cold and his legs looked funny where he must have been hit by a car, and he didn't look like Alfie any more. But the worst thing was, he'd died with a leaf in his mouth. He'd been so desperate for food, he'd been trying to eat a dandelion. He must've been so hungry – and we were only metres away, searching for him with plates of food, calling, *Alfie! Al-fie!* We'd been looking for him for three days, and all the time he'd been lying there getting hungrier and dying from an injury that maybe the vet could've fixed. If only he'd dragged himself home. That's what cats are like. Independent and stupid.

Mum thinks I'm stupid sometimes. The tree waves outside my window, beckoning me to climb it. I ought to get some exercise.

'Use the gym,' Mum says, 'instead of climbing that tree. Don't be afraid to ask for some help. They'll show you how to use the equipment.'

'That's what I'm afraid of. The tree's free,' I'm reminding her. 'At the gym you pay for induction. If I go back in September, I can use the school gym then.'

I'm supposed to go back part-time. Recovering from glandular fever can take months, plus you can set yourself back if you do too much at once.

'Keep yourself active in short bursts,' Mum says. 'You don't want to get depressed.'

'I'm not depressed, I'm nosy.'

'Get out for walks,' Mum says. 'It's stupid to live in the country and not get out for walks.'

'Climbing a tree isn't exercise?'

'You do more sitting than climbing,' Mum says. 'I wish you'd stay out of that tree.'

Every time the subject of the tree comes up, she has a go at me about doing some exercise. Every time exercise, viruses, illnesses or school phobias come up, she has a go at me about not sitting in the tree.

You can't win, I told Liv, but she had her head in a book.

Liv's reading *Wuthering Heights*, but she says it's pants. Over-heated and unrealistic, but we agreed that that was probably the point. Meanwhile, I know I'll get better. I won't stay wan and lonely like Emily Brontë, the author of *Wuthering Heights*, who probably could have done with a sister like Liv to set her straight when she moaned. I'm sticking to a yeast-free diet to help metabolize something-or-other, and give me more energy. So I'm putting away the Marmite, and getting out the jam, when Liv puts her head round the door. 'Guess what?'

'Surprise me.'

'Michael Paxman just told me he saw Luke Couch hosing Hodge.'

'When?'

'Last week. Michael said he soaked him.'

'*That's* why he came in wet. Luke hosed Paxman's garden after he washed Mrs Oliff's car – but Hodge came in wet again, Tuesday . . .'

'Does it matter when?' Liv says, in a hard voice. 'He's not going to get away with deliberately hosing our cat.'

It had to have something to do with the jet of water that Luke sent into the Paxmans' garden last Sunday. I'd thought I'd seen Mr Paxman telling Luke off. But Luke had handed Mr Paxman a card. They seemed to be agreeing on something. Plus Mr Paxman hates Hodge. Maybe it all added up.

'He might have asked Luke to do it.'

'Who?' Liv says.

'Mr Paxman.'

'Why?'

'Keep Hodge off his bird table?'

Funny how Luke Couch comes up smelling of roses from any situation. Take Mrs Oliff. He only got to wash her car in the first place because he messed it up. She gives him a lift and he spills a litre of milk in her footwell. 'Don't worry,' he says. 'I'll clean it up. Wash your car as well.'

That's how Danny tells it. Danny reads books. He's different from Luke. More *empathetic*. Danny says 'empathetic' means you respond to other people. You couldn't tell Mrs Oliff that. Mrs Oliff thinks Luke's wonderful.

'*What* a marvellous shine,' she says, when she comes out to pay him. I know, I listen sometimes. 'Never mind the change – I suppose you do quite well out of cleaning cars?'

'Well enough,' Luke says. He sees the old bird needs to chat. 'Mr Oliff all right today?'

'Mr Oliff's not very well. A hospital appointment, you know . . .'

'Least it's clean, to go in.'

'What is?'

'The car. To drive Mr Oliff into hospital.'

'Actually, a volunteer calls for him,' Mrs Oliff says. 'I suppose some cars are easier to wash than others?'

'Small ones is easier,' Luke says.

'I suppose you use a special car-wax?'

'Trade secret,' Luke winks.

'I've tried a shammy-leather myself,' says Mrs Oliff. 'But I end up just making marks.'

'Leather off when it's dry,' Luke advises. 'That way you don't get smears.'

He's actually quite kind to Mrs Oliff. Hard to believe he'd hose Hodge – or would he?

'Least it might cure him,' I'm telling Liv.

'Of what?'

'Going over the road.'

'Hodge, you mean. Thought you meant Luke,' Liv says.

'I think Mrs Oliff's lonely.'

'And?'

'That's why she has her car washed. Luke's actually quite nice to her.'

'Luke's nice to himself,' Liv says.

But still Mrs Oliff likes to chat with him. Other probably quite lonely people relying on Loony Luke's Carwash include Rosie Startup, Don Fisher, Mr Masterson and Mrs Venables down by the forge. Luke works his way through the village, finishing with Geoff Roland's Impreza at Vine Cottage, where the village officially ends. Commuters are Luke's bread-and-butter. The last thing an office manager like Rosie Startup wants to do on a weekend is to hose out the cow-poo from the wheel-trim of her Y-reg acid-green Micra.

I know when he's doing a carwash, even if I'm not up the tree. First you see the flood of water tailing off down the road. You'll hear the clunk of his buckets, and pretty soon Luke appears round the bend by White Cottage, shiny and pink like a bar of soap, his T-shirt stuck to his back. Everyone waves as he passes. Mrs Oliff watches him go. He gives her a wave with a five-pound note and swings off down the road. What a ray of sunshine. I wouldn't put it that way. That's the way my mother puts it.

'He's got charm, I'll give him that,' Mum says a couple of days later. '"Loony Luke's Carwash" – didn't he do a carwash last year?'

'I hope the reservoir can spare the water,' Dad grunts over his paper. 'You could irrigate an African village with the runoff from one of his jobs.'

'You know Luke put the hose on Hodge. He isn't charming at all.' I'm setting them straight. 'Michael Paxman told Liv he did it deliberately.'

'I said they could,' Mum says. 'At least, I told Michael Paxman that a short burst from the hose might stop Hodge hanging around their bird table.'

'Poor old Hodgie,' Liv says.

'You told the Paxmans they could hose our cat?' I can't believe she did that.

'Yes,' Mum says, 'but Michael said he wouldn't do it.'

'But he can't wait to tell Liv that he thinks he saw Luke do it. He probably *did*, accidentally. Or maybe Mr Paxman wanted him to, who knows?'

'You've lost me,' Mum says.

'Michael Paxman hates Luke. Maybe it all adds up.'

'Does he?' my mother says. 'Why?'

'He teases Michael ragged at the bus stop.'

'And no one helps Michael?'

'You don't understand.' She really doesn't. 'No one can help anyone at the bus stop. It's a jungle out there.'

'Come off it,' Liv says. 'Luke hoses anything. What are you defending him for?'

'It sounds to me as if Michael Paxman's trying to make Luke look bad.' Everyone turns to look at Dad.

'He doesn't need Michael to make him look bad. He does that all by himself,' Liv says.

'He *does* use a lot of water.' Dad frowns.

'He does actually tease his brother – but he's good with Mrs Oliff . . .'

'Make up your mind,' Liv says. 'Luke Couch, nice or not? Betting starts now.'

'Luke's all right,' my mother says. 'Everyone teases their brother. He may be a bit of a Jack the Lad, but whatever it is, he's got it.'

Whatever it is, I hope he deserves it. No need to make him out to be worse than he is, but everything falls into Luke's lap. He never seems to have to try for it.

Last night he walks under the tree, too busy looking at something to give me the usual clever comment or ear-splitting whistle. I'm holding my breath as he walks underneath. What's so absorbing, he can't look up? Even the leaves stand still.

I might have known it would be money.

He must have had sixty quid in his hand. The way people pay him round here, he'll be Mr Millionaire before he even leaves school. They probably think he's funny and hard-working – one of them, in fact. Luke Couch isn't so Loony as not to lower his prices now and then. He'll even throw in a free car fragrancer, so long as it's Alpine Meadow. Danny said Luke got a free box of Alpine Meadow car fragrancers from Kramer's garage last year, and he's still getting rid of them now.

Everyone you see whose car has been Luked, rides round with a car fragrancer shaped like a pine tree attached to their mirror. So he wins people over easily. Does a good job, as well. He may be funny and charming. But sixty quid already, and summer holidays to come — do they *have* to go over the top?

Chapter 5

That mad bat Sylvie Bickle was in the tree again this morning when me and Dan went to school.

'Hey, Luke,' she goes, 'hosed any cats lately?'

'Ha, ha, funny,' I'm saying. 'Got any birds in your hair?' Dunno why I said that, couldn't think of what to say. Only three weeks of school left now, so she won't have so much to nose about soon. Week after next, we'll be laughing. Summer holidays mean business opportunities. Good time to expand the carwash.

'Off to school to do nothing?' she goes and shouts after us.

'Don't throw your teddies out of the pram just because school won't have you.'

'Least I'm not cruel to animals.'

'Least I don't think I'm a bird up a tree. Don't lay an egg, will you?'

'Leave it alone,' Danny says.

Danny hates to mix it. Anything for a quiet life, the reason he and Sad Man Paxman are borderline Sad together.

I told him he'd get infected. 'What d'you mean?' Danny goes. Paxman's a creep, I'm telling him. Why, Danny goes, because he reads books? No, because he looks like he does, I'm telling Dan. Hang around with him much more, you'll get stuck like it.

Danny reads books secretly. You'd never catch him up the bus stop with *World At War*. Don't catch Paxman with it either, now I stuffed it in the postbox. 'Wise up, Paxman,' I told him. 'The war ended years ago.'

'Fifty-six years ago, to be exact,' Paxman goes, the reason why I hate him. People who think they're so clever really get on my nerves. Sylvie Bickle, up the tree, thinks she knows so much.

Coming home that day, she gets me again. 'Saw you washing Mrs Oliff's car the other day.'

'And?'

'You didn't polish it off.'

'What would you know?'

'More than you think.' She swings a leg, bites an apple. 'I see what you do round the village.'

'Mind your own business, why don't you?'

'The way you do, you mean?'

'What's that supposed to mean, you nosy GIT?'

Liv swings by and goes in the house, just when I'm saying GIT. Good going, Luke. Really cool. You wouldn't think stick-legs up the tree would have a sister like Liv. Bix's sister Liv – long hair, really fit, goes out with Matt Kramer, Sixth Form next year, so don't even think about it – always walks by herself. 'Hey,' I said once, 'what's the hurry?' But she didn't even look back.

'You didn't put any polish on it,' Bix goes.

'What?' The door slams as Liv goes in.

'Mrs Oliff's car. "Full Wax Finish", your card says. Trade descriptions could get you.'

'You think you're so clever, you don't know nothing about it.' Why should I explain the wax-in-the-washing-water shortcut to Nose of the Year up the tree? I remember being in class with her and she thought she knew everything then. 'Coming on like you know everything, just because you're good at English.'

'I'm *not* good at English.' She acts surprised. 'What makes you think I am?'

'Trade descriptions could get you,' I put on her voice.

'You don't polish off.'

'*You* say.'

'*And* you hosed our cat.'

'You're mad, you are,' I'm telling her.

'Come on,' says Dan, 'we're missing good telly.'

'I'm not the stirrer around here,' she goes.

'Too busy up the monkey club.' I'm doing my mad chimp impression, and Danny's dragging me off.

'*I've* seen you pushing Ben Dent,' she shouts, and that does it.

'You nosy cow! You think you're so clever –'

I'm in the hedge now, kicking her tree.

'Get down,' Dan goes. 'Luke, leave it!'

'– who d'you think you *are?*'

Danny drags me off, and then it's a normal evening, except now I know Liv thinks I suck, after Gorilla Girl probably slagged me off. She thinks I mixed it with Ben Dent.

The Ben Dent thing was ages ago. No one even remembers it now, 'cept for Big Brother up the tree. Now I just said GIT in the road. Liv must think I'm a div. Danny pinned me down once and asked me why she mattered so much. She doesn't matter, I told him. What d'you think I am, stupid?

I can think about her, can't I? Except that now when Liv passes, she'll think I'm crap. Liv thinking I'm all right means I don't have to try to impress anyone else. If it doesn't make sense, don't worry. It doesn't make sense to me. When Liv walks down the road, nothing ever makes sense, and I can't think of anything to say, so sometimes I dump on Paxman, for a laugh. Sometimes she smiles if I say something funny, just the corner of her mouth. I can be really funny. When she's watching, I go a bit mad. That's the problem, Danny says. Liv being there makes me worse.

Now I blew it big time, with the GIT in the road and the Ben Dent thing. Plus the carwash is embarrassing. I'm hoping Liv Bickle never even remembers I do the carwash, after I stuffed up delivering my card.

The evening I designed my latest card, I was out watching Dan nut a basket – he's so crap, he can't shoot a hoop – when Mum comes out and goes, 'Why not design a new business card?'

'What for?'

'The carwash.'

'Good one,' I'm letting her know, stealing the ball off Dan, netting a three-pointer from the side of the chicken coop to show him how it should be done.

Later, I'm sitting in front of the computer, calling up last year's business card and wondering how I got any business when my card was so rubbish, when Mum goes, 'Why not try Autodesign? You might find a picture of a car. Jazz up your card a bit.'

'Maybe I need a new name. Crazy Couch's Carwash. Mad Mark's Carwash. Manic Wash 'n' Wax —'

'Stick with "Loony Luke",' Dad goes. 'Everyone thought it was funny.'

In the end I stick with the old card and drop in a picture of a car and alter the border a bit. Under the car I slot in a new line: *Loony Luke's Back and Better Than Ever — Mad Prices!! Full Wash and Wax!! Two Cars Cleaned for the Price of One, Summer Holiday Offer!!!!'*

'How will that work?' Danny goes.

'Because I'll do it fast, for not very long, then have loads of new customers, obviously.' Danny doesn't know a thing. 'Don't know a thing, do you?'

Later, Dad helps me print out.

Next day, after tea, I hit Orchard Close with my new business cards. Orchard Close is where Liv lives. Then I remember the dingbat as I'm going up the Bickles' drive. She's probably in the tree right now. Watching me all the time.

In fact, she opens the door. I swear she saw me coming.

'Yes,' she says, 'what is it?'

'Carwash.'

'What?' She stares at me like I'm mad.

'Carwash — take a card.'

Liv swings down the stairs. 'Luke,' she says. 'What are you doing?'

'Giving out cards,' says the dingbat, like I just told her a secret.

'I'm doing the carwash – take one.'

Liv takes my card and reads it. 'Back and Better Than Ever.'

'Two for One. Cheap summer rates.'

'Loony Luke. Like the name.'

'I used it before.'

'Yes,' she goes, 'you did.' She looks at me directly, like she never did before, and nothing makes sense as usual, and I don't know what I'm doing there.

'Full wash and wax, any time, just gimme a bell, gotta go.' Looking good there, Luke, babbling like an idiot in front of Liv.

I can hear them laughing as I walk away. The dingbat's laughing, anyway. Top business move, Luke, giving out carwash cards to people who don't have cars. Move over, Richard Branson, it's Businessman of the Year.

I stuff the rest of my business cards through letterboxes up through the village, missing out Nathan Beddoes' house, though he'll catch up with it anyway and give me a hard time about it. At least the name's a laugh. Loony Luke's Carwash, it's a joke – what, me serious about anything? Everyone thinks it's kid's stuff. It's child's play to take the money, with no competition. I'm telling you, it works. Funny's the way to play it.

Next morning, the Bickles are up at the bus stop

together, for a major change of heart. You never see them together, let alone Bix in school.

'Starting school again, are we?'

The dingbat stares at me. 'No.'

'Don't rush into it now.'

'What do you care?' Bix says.

Liv moves, but I can't see her face. I'm guessing I should lay off, but I still want to know. 'Why are you going in then?'

'Collecting work, like you need to know.' She turns and gives Liv daggers. 'Like Liv couldn't pick it up for me.'

'Between you and Mr Fowler,' Liv says. 'Nothing to do with me.'

The school bus comes round the corner like an elephant with bits falling off it.

'Parents get my card?' I get near Liv in the queue.

'Card?'

'The carwash. I redesigned it.'

'I'll pass it on.' She gets on the bus and sits down smelling of apples, and buries her face in a book.

'Cheers.'

I thought she might say, 'No problem,' but she doesn't look up from her book, and Beddoes is taking the mick, and I have to move on down the aisle. Don't know what I was expecting. She liked the name, 'Loony Luke'. I thought she might be impressed by the new business card. So I wasn't too smooth when I brought it round. I got off my backside and did it, didn't I?

I thought she might admire enterprise. I thought she

might notice there was more to me than Funny. She looked at me once, on the doorstep, like I existed.

Now it's like I went away again.

She said five words to me: Card, I'll, Pass, It and On. But still Liv's face doesn't show that she's impressed by business enterprise at all.

And this was before I called her sister a git.

How much worse is it now, after Gorilla Girl told her I duffed up Ben Dent? The bit she didn't see is when Ben Dent duffed up Danny first. I only straightened him out, but who cares anyway, except that it makes me mad as hell to know what they think about me, and even madder that I care.

Chapter 6

Loony Luke's Carwash. Liv remembers it now.

His second card reminds her of the first time she heard about Loony Luke's Carwash, last summer, through the almost imperceptible sound of a card falling softly on the doormat . . .

She's alone in the house. The tree wags outside the window. She and Matt Kramer have been together for three months, and have just broken up. Again.

Pausing while applying mascara, Liv hears the letter-box snap and searches the darkness of the stairwell to see a lonely white card on the doormat. A little lonely – and jumpy – herself, she clumps downstairs to retrieve it. If only Matt had sent it, but no – instead the card announces some stupid local carwashing service:

Loony Luke! The Best Carwasher
In The South West

Mobile: 077778983451
Home: (03439) 830976
!!! INTRODUCTORY OFFER !!!
£3.00 per car, £4.00 per van, £6.00 Full Valet

The Best Carwasher in the South West. Just a modest claim then. 'Loony Luke's Carwash'. Brilliant name. *You know you want to hire me*, the card says between the lines — *What, no sense of humour?*

Liv's nose twitches. Enormous potential for a story. She can see it ballooning out like those elephant letters trumpeting prices across his card. Loony Luke — it's a gift. A story about a carwash, why not? 'Loony Luke's Carwash' wouldn't be *Romantic* at all, but you don't look a gift-horse in the mouth . . .

What would a gift-horse look like? Probably it would have medieval Lady-of-Shalott-type tapestries over its back, and a golden bridle. What would it be bringing? Matt on its back, with luck . . .

Since last summer, what had it brought her?

More pain than gain, if she's honest. More ups and downs with Matt than anyone had a right not to want or expect in a year and three months' being together, more off than on. A familiar, heavy mood settles over her heart, the gloom that Liv lives with now. The gloom feeds the Romantic phase she's going through in preparation for the start of her A Level Literature course in September. Romantic with a capital 'R' means poets who brood a lot about Nature, with a capital 'N'. Suffering is Romantic. So is opium addiction, heady poems dashed off at the summit of dangerous peaks, unrequited love, storms, brooding landscape, doomed youth and writing about things you don't know about, but can imagine after reading travel books.

Liv's written stories for as long as she can remember, usually imaginative pieces about people lost in the desert, parched wells, their dying thoughts, fingers clenching in death, wind obliterating their footsteps, etc., and she's suffered for her Art, which has to be Romantic.

Once she had a thing about the garden shed, and shut herself up to write in it, but the 'lantern' she'd improvised out of a plastic budgie bath with a lighted candle inside it had suddenly flared up on the wall and had taken off her eyebrows and frizzled her fringe and covered the story she was working on with flaming lumps of burning plastic. The parchment and sealing-wax phase in the cellar had involved minor burns, as well.

When Liv was nine or ten, she went through a phase of making quills from swans' feathers she found in the park, which had involved only minor cuts and oil on the living-room carpet. Then there was oak-apple ink, which involved bashing nails through oak-apples, which led to a few bashed fingers. Then there was the invisible-ink phase – scorched eyebrows again, this time from heating up lemon-juice writing on the gas ring, to show up the letters.

Liv hasn't had much luck with eyebrows, making it all the more amazing they're so sleek and well-defined now. Disfigurement for the sake of art has to be Romantic, though sacrificing your eyebrows looks a bit cold beside Byron's fight for Greek freedom. Lord Byron had thick black eyebrows and did mad things, but mostly he felt sorry for himself, the way Liv feels right now.

Not so sorry for Byron. But sorry for mad things she did.

Thinking about writing to Matt, unless it will make things worse, except how much worse can it be than breaking up yet again, Liv shapes perfect eyebrows with a tiny little brush. Loony Luke's new business card draws her eyes to it, despite her annoyance with it, herself and Luke.

Loony Luke's Carwash. Didn't she plan to write a story about that once? Liv tucks the card in the corner of the mirror and begins Superlashing her eyelashes, mouth open, eyes drawn to Loony Luke's announcement. *Two Cars Cleaned for the Price of One, Summer Holiday Offer!!* The second card's smarter, more confident. It's grown a computer-designed logo and a bad cartoon of a car. Best of all, as a welcome break, it shouts: Nothing to Do With Matt.

So the first time he leaves his card, she gets an idea. The second time, Liv looks at Loony Luke and decides she'll do something about it. The reawakening of the idea about writing a story called 'Loony Luke's Carwash' had really begun on the doorstep. She'd looked at him and thought, 'interesting', without knowing why.

Now what she had to do was obvious. Luke had stuffed his card in her hand and had run away in confusion. Bix had laughed a lot. Now it was vital *not to know too much about the real Luke.* All she needed was to watch him wash a few cars, to 'get' the carwashing business. A few funny stories about carwashing and her imagination would do the rest. Perfect, she thinks, Luke who? I don't know a thing about him. I can make him into anything I want. Use that funny story idea, take my mind off things I should do . . .

Liv takes the card downstairs and pins it on the kitchen noticeboard.

That evening the 'Luke' of a fictional carwash starts to grow in her mind. He balloons over the next few days into a monster of self-interest, likeable but flawed, hard on the outside, soft on the inside, with a lot to discover about himself and the world, especially his expectations of it. Before long, it never occurs to her, for some reason, that the Luke Couch of next door might not actually *be* the Loony Luke of Legend already snowing the village with cards in Liv's imagination, throwing out storylines from the carwash over the course of a sweltering summer . . .

On Saturday Liv throws the card casually on the kitchen table.

'Mum, see this card – want the car washed?'

'Loony Luke.' Lyn Bickle laughs. 'We'll give him a go, why not?'

Why not, indeed? No one else washes the car. Liv's initial deal with her mother, to wash the car now and then in exchange for future driving lessons, faded long ago. Time to call in a pro – lively, first-hand information to paint the carwash in *real* colours, the best way to set up a story. With the exception of Tiggy Biggelowe, all characters will be fictitious . . .

She should take up wearing a hat. Develop a few writer's rituals, like walking up to the café to write at the same table every day. Cultivate an eccentric image. Then they could point out her table: 'Yes, Olivia Bickle wrote here, at Kitty's

Kitchen, every day. Had the All Day Breakfast. Couldn't have written that classic, "Loony Luke's Carwash" without it.'

Liv feels sick at the thought of breakfast. She should get a summer holiday job, but she's sick at the thought of that too. 'So will you call him soon?' she says, returning to the matter in hand.

'Call who?'

'Loony Luke.'

'How soon would you like?' says Mrs Bickle.

So the day after Mrs Bickle rings him, Luke comes round with his buckets in get-it-over-with-quickly mode, not some legendary figure after all, just bog-standard Luke Couch from next door, shedding no glamour around him at all, and making stories seem silly. Crunching around on the gravel in wellies, snapping the wipers away from the wind-screen ready for washing, soaping his sponges and flinging on suds, Luke's yellow waterproof slides from pane to pane of the bubbled glass in the front door, and looms more yellowly as he passes.

Buckets, rags, cloths and bottles, Liv notes through the window. For the first time it occurs to her that cars don't stay clean by themselves. 'Noisy, isn't he?'

She heads for the door.

'Going out to watch?' Mrs Bickle intercepts her.

'Why not?'

'Better leave him to it. I think he likes it that way,' says Mrs Bickle, unusually sensitive to business enterprise and space for a Good Job Well Done.

Liv retires to the window. Leave it a moment. Keep it light. Don't ask too many questions.

After a while, comes a knock at the door. 'Where'd you keep the hose?' Luke mumbles, shiny with effort.

'I'm sorry?' Mrs Bickle frowns.

'Hose,' Luke says, again.

'Round the side of the house.' Fascinated by the way his potato head is flecked with foam, 'Want a hand?' Mrs Bickle shouts after him. She waits a moment for an indecipherable reply, and decides to leave him to it.

The hose whips round the corner like a live thing.

Liv watches from the window as Luke appears with the end of it and uses a dramatic amount of water, which will hopefully soak into the gravel before her father comes home. How could she have thought that Luke, or someone like him, could feature in a story? But he might be a mine of information. Do half the writing for her, if anything funny or colourful happened during the time he's been doing the carwash. He must hear gossip. See funny things. Read people's lives and characters from the lives and characters of their cars. Time to try to find out.

Shrugging on her denim jacket, Liv rounds the house with a letter, as though surprised on her way to the post-box. 'Oh . . . Luke – how's it going?'

Luke grunts. 'All right.'

'On to the shammy stage already?'

Luke grunts again, in a what's-it-look-like way.

His back doesn't look too promising. What's he got to be browned off about? When did she last speak to him?

With an effort, Liv remembers that he spoke to her on the bus. Something about passing on his business card to her parents. Well, she *had* passed on his card.

'I suppose you meet a lot of different people, doing the carwash,' Liv tries gamely, anyway. 'You must hear some funny stories.'

Luke shrugs. 'Not really.'

'Must be nice to see cars you've cleaned driving around.'

'Suppose.'

'Hard work.'

'Yeah.' Dramatic circles with the leather. Too busy to meet her eyes.

'Is there something the matter?'

'Depends.'

'What do you mean?'

'Bix say anything about me?'

'No,' Liv says, 'why would she?'

'Ben Dent pushed Danny first,' Luke says, even busier with his shammy than before. ''Case you think I'm rubbish.'

Liv attempts to digest this and fails. 'So some cars are worse to clean than others?'

'People keep asking me stuff.' Luke replaces the wipers against the windscreen and turns his attention to the wing mirrors. 'I just wash cars, all right?'

'Fine,' Liv says. 'Just showing an interest.' No source of material here then. Just another job for Loony Luke, button-lipped and almost annoyed with her for some reason, intent on finishing as fast as he can, on taking the money and running. Liv watches the leathering process move smoothly across the car. 'D'you like cleaning cars?'

'Not much.'

'Why do you do it then?' she asks, after a while.

'Why do you think – money.'

'Money for what?'

'Discman.' Luke flings the hose on the ground. 'I never meant what I said to Bix.'

'What did you say to Bix?'

Luke sweats from every pore. 'Shouting GIT in the road. And I never pushed Ben Dent before he *went and pushed Danny*.'

'I'm sure you didn't.' Liv looks at Luke. How peculiar he is. Almost angry that he has to explain himself. 'How long will it take you?' she asks.

'Do what?'

'To make enough for a discman?'

'Got enough for one already. And a mobile phone.'

Luke crunches round the side of the house to pull the hose round the corner and throw it down at the tap, where Liv's father will tutt a lot and grumpily coil it later. Liv watches as the end of it whips off round the corner like a snake with a sudden appointment.

Unwilling to knock at the door for payment while Liv's around, Luke finds his buckets need cleaning.

'Loony Luke's Carwash, makes a great title.' Liv can sense that he wants her to go. So moody with her – why? 'Might have to use it in a story sometime.'

Luke makes a grunt between 'yeah' and 's'pose'.

'I wouldn't make it anything like you.'

Luke finds a spot that he missed on the other side of the car. Liv gets out of his way. 'I'd just like to use the name, would you mind?'

Luke disappears behind the car. A squeaking sound announces some work with the shammy.

'That is, if I ever get round to it.'

More squeaking sounds from the shammy.

'Well, I'd better post this letter.' Liv backs off with her letter. 'You missed a bit.'

Luke's head pops up.

'By the wing mirror – there.'

Liv leans her head against the stubbly, encrusted red paint of the postbox embedded in the side of White Cottage. Luke hadn't acknowledged her departure by so much as a glance or a shrug. He didn't know what she was talking about. Stories didn't figure in his world.

A wave of nausea washes over her. For a moment she thinks she might faint. Sitting down on the wall, she reviews the conversation and thinks. The grunt between 'yeah' and 's'pose' was good – it gives her permission, surely, to borrow the name of the carwash?

Fiction, after all, isn't it? The grunt is all she needs.

'You must admit, it's clean.' Mrs Bickle examines the car when Loony Luke has been paid and praised, and has gone off, jingling his money. 'Shiniest I've ever seen it.'

'Light rub with Premier Turtle Wax,' Bix says.

'You didn't see him wash the car,' Liv says.

'Seen him wash millons of cars.'

The secrets of the carwash stay with Liv most of the day. Lots of welly with the leather. Pay attention to lights, wings and bonnet. But the rest of the process, and Luke himself, remain a mystery.

'Is someone saying Luke pushed Ben Dent?' Liv asks, later that day.

'Saw him do it,' Bix says.

'But Luke says Ben Dent pushed Danny first. He's really angry about it.'

'He would say that,' Bix says.

'Why does he care what I think?'

'You work it out,' Bix says.

The funny stories Liv had hoped for remain a mystery as well – so much the better, as now she'll be making them up. Still the mind of Loony Luke is different from the way she'd imagined her hero might be. 'He only does it for the money,' she says, over tea.

'What else would he do it for?' Mrs Bickle raises her eyebrows.

'I mean, money's all he thinks about.'

'You surprise me,' Lyn Bickle says.

'He might've coiled the hose, instead of just throwing it down,' Mr Bickle grumbles that night. 'And he's flooded the drive.'

'You're right about the water,' Liv says. 'I think he likes using the hose.'

Later she opens a document on the computer and heads it 'Loony Luke's Carwash'. It's going well, for a while. An outline, a bit of dialogue – 'What?'

Bix enters the room. Says: 'Feathers.'

'I'm writing,' Liv says. 'Go away.'

'Like the Brontës,' says Bix. 'I'm up the tree being alone, you're indoors writing stories.'

'What are you talking about?'

'Sisters,' Bix says.

'And?'

'Feathers.'

'What feathers?'

'Park feathers you put in the cupboard.'

'Years ago,' Liv says. 'What d'you want those old things for?'

'Because I just do.'

Liv shrugs. 'Help yourself, if you can find them.'

Her sister's bony behind bobs in and out of the loft-space opening through a cupboard door into her bedroom, as Liv pegs on with her story, not much more than a changing idea, as yet. Forgotten objects and musty-smelling bin bags emerge from the cupboard as Bix climbs in and disappears. Tennis racquets, teddies, stools, books, tents, table football . . .

Liv gets up and hovers. 'Must you drag all that stuff out?' she asks her sister's behind. The parchment and sealing-wax years rise up in her mind's eye, as bits and pieces from years ago tumble out of bags on to the floor, like a waiting tide of memory kept back by the cupboard door and now in full flood – a flood of fusty smells and disturbing tugs at the heart.

'Remember the stuff in this suitcase?' Bix drags it out anyway.

'No, I don't,' Liv says. 'And please can you put it away?'

Liv shuts down the computer and scribbles a reminder to herself: *Get Belt in Town. Don't Even Think About Crying.* The chain-belt that Matt had promised to buy her for her birthday – now she would buy it for herself, as a symbol that Life Would Go On. Tears well up at the thought of the night of the break-up, the last in a line of break-ups, since when everything had been coloured gloomy and broken. Too much to hope he'd remember a card. Life goes on, her mother had said. Writing always cheers you up. Why not write something funny?

'Here they are!'

'What?'

'Park feathers!' Bix triumphantly drags out a smelly box of feathers. 'There's more here than I thought there'd be.'

Liv crosses the cluttered floor and peers in.

'They niff a bit, don't they? Happy now you rubbished my room?'

'Remember when you used to collect these from Lakey Park?' Bix looks at Liv through a feather. 'You had that friend, Christine? When you did that secret club in the cellar, when the budgie bath caught fire?'

'That was the shed,' Liv says, coldly. 'Can you clear up now and *go*?'

After the accumulated lumber of years has been pushed back into the hot, timber-smelling loft space, and Bix has departed with her box, memories still claim Liv's thoughts. Rescuing a forgotten greyish quill from the carpet, she smooths it between her fingers. How white they'd come up when you washed them. A splash of detergent in a bucket outside – a row of creamy feathers, drying in the sunshine, in no time. Fun at Christine's house. The Ingoldsby Legends, frightening them under the sheets. The birch at the bottom of the garden they used to climb together. Lakey Park, a stone's throw away, with its boats, playground, zoo, the twisted pine you could sit in, the discarded swans' feathers waiting at the edge of the lake for someone to collect them, the frozen pond in winter, an adventure waiting to happen. The fascination of those perfect, creamy feathers, bobbing in nooks round the lake, the lure of finding the biggest one, wanting to collect more and more . . .

Christine of the plaits and hairband had lived near Park Gates in a comfortable sunshiny house with a large piano. Her neighbour, whose house bordered the park, had allowed Christine and her friends access to the park through her garden. They'd flip up a couple of loose stakes in the fence, and bob into Lakey Park – a secret way in to the wilds of the dank bamboo thicket behind the shed housing the miniature train, in one thrillingly change-filled step.

Liv and Christine had collected the smooth white feathers trapped in crannies around the lake, bringing them home to wash and sort. Their fascinating hook-and-eye fibres would separate with a tearing sound, then knit together again. Too much detergent would destroy their waterproofing. You only needed a bit. The biggest feathers made quill-pens, seriously blotchy when you used them, adding romance to letters or 'documents' sealed with sealing wax or 'aged' with coffee or tea. Sometimes a girl named Vicky would come and help wash feathers, though Vicky was quite annoying.

Still, one day Liv and Christine had taken a paddle boat out on the lake and had buried a jar on Swans Island with a note screwed tightly inside it that said that Christine, Vicky and Olivia would be friends for ever and ever, and would never, ever part . . .

Tears, again. For heaven's sake.

'Stupid, smelly old feathers,' Liv shouts across the landing at the bedroom door that says *Sylvia*. 'What do you want them for, anyway?'

Liv watches telly that night as the light fades slowly over the Chapel and a lawn-mower buzzes outside. Long, droning summer evenings – what are they for? They only make you remember summer evenings long ago . . . Maybe she wouldn't know Christine of the thick fingers and red hair-band now, if she fell over her in the street. I loved her like a sister, Liv realizes, but what does that *mean*, after losing touch? Maybe she's leaving school this summer. Getting a job. Or staying on like me, planning to go to college or university, never thinking about, never remembering, the day we corked a message in a jar that swore we'd never lose touch. *I promise we'll always be friends, for ever and ever and ever . . .*

Liv broods in bed that night. Nothing's ever what you think it'll be, especially relationships. Funny how people are different inside, from outside. Especially boys. Matt's a mystery – so is Luke Couch. Do they have to act like aliens? It's hard to understand. Of course Luke's point of view was a key to making the carwash interesting. Of course he was going to be – different. But moody and hostile? Maybe even Luke Couch has hidden depths, when he's not in a mood. There must be some background there somewhere, assuming there's more going on than the urge for a discman . . . Luke's silence is puzzling. She could be underestimating her sources. But somehow, after the carwash, Liv begins to doubt it. Maybe there's nothing to find out. Matt's tired of going out with her, and that's that, no third party involved. Luke Couch just washes cars and takes no interest in his customers. No stories anywhere, just life going on, because it has to.

Liv feels weariness creep through her bones. Only half-past ten. Why is she so tired, these days?

Chapter 7

Accounts Ledger, Profit and Loss
Business name: Loony Luke's Carwash

Loo-king good. Business name, Loony Luke. How professional does my name on a bookkeeping ledger make me look? Double-entry bookkeeping? No problemo, now Dad showed me how to fill in the columns. Feels like a proper business with my professional name on the books.

The last thing we professionals want is people washing their cars. Yesterday we're coming off the school bus, walking down the road, after Paxman ran off blubbing because somebody took his war book – not me – when there's Mrs Jamieson on the corner only *washing her own car.*

'She's doing my job, I'm not happy,' I'm saying loudly as I come down the road, so Mrs Jamieson looks up and laughs.

'You're too expensive,' she says, her fault for tipping me last time.

Time for new page – I'm heading it 'Spring Point Garage'. Watch out for big, fat profits, now I got the

Kramer concession. I went up the garage last night. Found old man Kramer and said, 'Remember me from last year?'

He looks at me. 'Luke?'

'Loony Luke – the carwash, last summer, remember?'

He looks at me again. 'How could I forget?'

'I was wondering if I could do the carwash here again this year?'

'Getting a drive-through put in,' he grunts.

'A drive-through?'

'Automatic carwash,' old man Kramer mumbles. 'Won't be no business this year.'

Then my lucky day in disguise, Matt Kramer, comes out of the office. Old man Kramer's son, Matt – stubble, leather jacket, Lower Sixth, went out with Sara Bedwell and Liv Bickle, tools around in his Escort, thinks he's It – looks at me and goes, 'Luke – touting for business?'

'Carwash,' I'm telling him. What's it to you?

'Told him we got a drive-through being installed,' grunts cave-man Kramer.

'Not till September, surely?' Matty-boy oils, working out how he can use this. 'I'm sure we can fit in a schoolboy carwash over the holidays. How many days would you like?'

'Five be all right?' I'm trying.

'You got to keep out of the way,' the old man rumbles. 'Can't wash cars while people fill up.'

'Why not, it worked last year.'

'People come in for petrol, they don't like to wait for a carwash.'

'So give them a coffee. I'll make it.'

'*And* wash their cars?'

'Why not?'

The old man scratches his head. 'Your funeral,' he goes, ambling off to serve a customer.

'What did you pay us last year?' Matt goes, like he can't remember.

'Ten per cent of my take.'

'It went up to twenty per cent,' he goes, like Businessman of the Year.

'That's almost a quarter of what I make.'

'Take it or leave it,' he goes.

'I brought in business, last year – remind Mr Kramer, shall I?'

'It's not negotiable, Couch,' Matt goes, like he's a big wheel, or something.

'Fifteen per cent and a forecourt pitch.' I make like I'm going to check with the old man.

'All right,' he goes, 'deal. We'll compromise.'

'I need a table and a chair.'

'That's my problem?'

'Plus use of the power hose.' Compromise with *that*.

'Whatever,' he goes. 'Do your thing. Just don't let me hear about it.'

Just hand me the profits, you mean. Thinks he can fleece me. He's so wrong. Cross that bridge when I come to it.

Old man Kramer's all right, pity about the offspring. The old man waves to me over the till as I go, but he waves to everyone anyway, and he probably doesn't know who I am. The old man's pretty short-sighted, takes him a while to get to know you. We got on all right last year, even though I wasn't up the garage that long before the holidays ended. Washing cars fast at the pumps is hard work, but the Kramer concession is solid gold. Pity Matt Kramer knows it.

'All right if I start next Saturday?' I stick my head round the shop door, but the old man's too busy yakking to a customer to notice what I'm saying.

I'll probably have to explain what I'm doing again when I prop up my sign next Saturday. Danny said I should have a sign – 'Spring Point Carwash'. Why not?

'You can make it then,' I said.

'Make it yourself,' Danny said, getting out his magic markers and sitting down to make me a sign before I said anything else. I might nick a chair and the old table from the back of the barn to prop it up, when he's made it. Take up the old rags and brushes. Wash out my sponges, give the old shammy a treat . . .

That's next Saturday sorted, so I can work up the garage concession before the holidays start. Meanwhile the carwash is cooking with gas round the village.

Under 'Profit' I'm entering eight quid from Barry at the Post Office for washing two of his vans. Hubbard the Newsagent, four quid. A couple of Two-for-One Summer Offers makes it eighteen quid altogether, plus Angie Fisher's Metro and Nicola Hand's Honda Civic – plus a fiver from Liv's mum makes it twenty-nine quid, not bad for less than four hours' work. And more where that came from.

Liv's mum likes me, I reckon, a bit more than Liv does anyway. I tried to set the Ben Dent thing straight, but why did I have to be in a mood when she finally thawed and talked to me? I don't care whether she talks to me. I just don't want her to think I'm a div.

It's not like I fancy her or anything. Why would I let on I fancied her, when Liv's a Year Eleven? Everyone fancies her.

You don't want to let on you like anyone, up at the bus stop. Specially not someone like Liv. Matt Kramer can like Liv. Matt Kramer went out with Liv, still does, some people say. Why would she go out with muscle-head? Women, they're aliens.

Liv's pretty cool to everyone.

Now she thaws for some reason, and I have to be in a mood, but what does she think? Those questions about the carwash. Chatting and wanting to know stuff, like Mrs Oliff, and everyone else.

What do they think, it's fun? It's just cleaning muck off, polishing cars. Why is everyone so interested in the carwash?

So Liv got me the job washing her mum's car, that gives her the right to ask me to spill my guts about the business? She's probably laughing right now – asking me stuff about things I hear, why I like to wash cars, wanting to use my name, as if. What is she on? I'm asking Danny.

'She and Matt Kramer cooked this up,' I'm telling Danny. 'He wants to know what I'm charging this year, he can come right out and ask me.'

'She's not going out with Kramer any more,' Danny says. 'Paxman says they finished.'

'Paxman – what would he know?'

'She isn't spying for Kramer,' Danny says. 'She wants to use your name in a story, what's your problem?'

Now he puts it that way . . .

'Why would she want to do that?'

Danny shrugs. 'Looking for something to write about.'

'Why?'

'Suppose she likes writing stories.'

'Why?'

'Reckon she likes you,' Dan goes.

'You having a laugh?'

'No, she is.'

Now Liv's mum's been going round the village telling everyone what a good job I did on their car. People as far as Alfington are booking me up for next week.

With the Kramer concession and a pitch up at the White Hart pub on weekends, we could be looking at a trip to the Odyssey catalogue store and a discman in a week or two, maybe even Gamestation Two, thanks very much, horse dung in the road, mucking up everyone's motors . . .

'Liv said it makes a great title – Loony Luke's Carwash.'

'Mad for it,' Danny goes. 'You're in there,' he goes, laughing his head off. Laughing-boy's jealous, all right. All Danny does is read, with his head up close to the book. He watches videos with his nose up close to the telly. Sometimes he swaps them with Paxman. That's what he calls a life.

Now he's jealous the business took off and I'm building something up for myself, unlike Dr Dankenstein, curse of anything breakable.

'Dad know you broke the quad yet?' That wipes the smile off his face. Danny's latest disaster.

'Dunno what you mean,' Disaster-Man mumbles.

'I think I'd better tell him. It's not fair to keep it quiet.'

'So she wants to put *you* in a story?' Danny says, changing the subject.

'Not me, my name.'

'What did she want to know?'

'I don't know, do I? Stories about the carwash.'

'Background.' Like he'd know. 'She needs a carwash in a story.'

'Think you're clever . . .'

'Not hard next to you . . .'

'Final answer?'

'Final answer.' I smack Danny a bit. After I've got him pinned on the bed, 'So what should I tell her?' I'm asking him.

'Who?'

'Liv, if she wants stuff for stories.'

Danny tries to nut me. 'Gerroff or I'll shout for Mum!'

'If Mum was in, you would.'

'I'll fart you off,' he says, going red, trying to heave me off him.

'Think she wants stuff about cars?'

'And washing them, I'm guessing.' Danny tenses but nothing comes out.

'What should I tell her then?'

'Something gory,' he goes. 'Someone stuck in the engine.'

'Accidents, you mean?'

'Cat on telly this morning. Leg got caught in a fan-belt. Had to be cut off.'

'The fan-belt?'

'The leg.'

I take my arm off his neck. 'Where'd you hear it again?'

'Told you. Breakfast TV.' Danny lets one rip. *Perrr-ippp!* 'You need dramatic stuff. Gorier the better.'

'You reckon?'

'Human interest, that kind of thing. Your uncle lost his leg.'

'He did?'

'Get out some war films for ideas. Then make up how it happened.'

'What's that got to do with the carwash?'

'So make it a car crash, whatever. All that meaning-of-life stuff. Anything gross'll do.'

When I finally let Danny up, he runs to the door. 'Like anything *you* say's interesting, you stupid, ignorant moron!' he bellows so loudly his face goes red, and bits of spit hit the wall.

I'm up like lightning. 'Shout at me, would you?'

Danny takes off with a bullet.

'Spanner! Dingus! Fartpants!' I'm on his tail like a rocket, but he's locked himself in the bathroom.

'Got in the shower before you!' he sings. 'Pleased you let me in first?'

'Swivel on it,' I tell him, going back to mess up his bed. Then I mess up his war films. Oh no, they'll be out of order! Quite a little Paxman, in secret. He's only got them alphabetized – *Gump. Platoon. Ryan.* Danny's got 'em all.

Later, when I get in the shower myself, and find Danny's put grit in the soap, I'm thinking Danny's right.

I don't know any good stories about the carwash, so I'd better make some up. Need something quite unusual. Cat in the engine might do it. Uncle in the engine, even better. I'm competing here with Paxman in the storytelling stakes. Paxman spills his guts about everything to anyone who'll listen, 'specially Liv.

Now I come to think about it . . .

Liv asks everyone questions. She asked spoddy Dominic Wellington all about his cousin last week. His cousin's a dancer in London. She asked Nathan Beddoes about his uncle, who's this famous fish chef or something. Where does he get his recipes? she wants to know on the school bus. How many dishes does he cook every day, how often does he change them, would he ever do anything else? Nathan thinks it's his lucky day, but, next day, Liv ignores him. Bedders thinks she's messing with his mind. He doesn't know it's background.

Now I'm starting to think that the best way to learn about the carwash would be to start washing cars. Have a shammy, Liv. Want some funny stories? Try some work experience. Apply to me, Loony Luke. I'm imagining how it might go, when Danny snaps me in the head with a towel as I'm coming out of the bathroom.

'Mum! Luke just flicked me with a towel!' He runs downstairs like his pants are on fire to tell Mum I did it to him. Then, when I set her straight, it'll look like I'm lying.

Nice one, Danny, grow up. For someone who discusses filmic technique with Sad Man over the road, he acts pretty childish, sometimes.

Still thinking about Liv and the carwash . . .

Work experience, why not? I'm picturing showing Liv my shammy technique as I'm stuffing Danny's pillowcase with the smelliest socks I can find. Crude, but effective, I find. Once I stuffed a blister pack of raw mince in the back of Danny's cupboard. It smelled like the most disgusting thing you can imagine after three or four days. After a couple of weeks, it got so he couldn't go in his room. He had to turn everything out. Finally he found it. 'Cottage pie,' I told him.

We haven't eaten mince since. Socks are a safer bet. Evil, but slow-release. I'm picturing Liv saying, 'Luke, you're a pro, I never thought of melting wax in the washing-water', as I'm closing the door on Dan's room, and taking a triple-layer sarnie to mine.

The work-experience idea keeps me thinking all night. If it's still looking good in the morning, next time I see her, I'll ask her.

Chapter 8

'Sorry about the other day. I was in a bit of a mood. If you want to know what carwashing's like, how about work experience?'

'What?' Liv Bickle's so taken aback to have Luke Couch speak to her at all at the bus stop, that she doesn't hear what he says.

'Work experience – for background, right?' Luke Couch tips her a wink.

Liv wafts her hand. 'Eggbreath.'

'Sorry.' Luke isn't much abashed. 'So what do you think?'

'About what?'

'Like I said. Work experience.'

Liv Bickle looks at Luke. She can't be bothered with him now and, in any case, she has other, more serious things to think about. 'What are you talking about?'

'I'll show you the carwash,' Luke offers, even more eggily this time. 'Want to work for me then?'

The bus stop strains to hear the fulfilment of this fantasy.

'Why would I want to work for you?' Liv says.

'So you can put the carwash in a story,' Luke explains, patiently. 'I got the Kramer concession.'

'The what?'

'A carwashing pitch up at Spring Point Garage. Worth a mint over the holidays.'

'And I could be a part of that?' Liv puts her hand on her heart. She doesn't mean to be nasty, but what is he thinking?

Luke's face drops. 'Yeah. If you want.'

Someone whistles in the background. 'Go, Luke.' Luke glances round, embarrassed, but something's wrong. She should be grateful by now, asking which bucket to bring.

'So do you?' he says.

'Do I what?' Liv turns icy eyes on him.

'Want to do carwashing with me?'

'At my ex-boyfriend's dad's garage?'

'Now you put it like that . . .' Luke admits.

'Just leave me alone,' Liv hisses. 'Think you can manage that?'

Luke subsides in confusion. What went wrong this time?

'Went well, I thought,' says Beddoes. 'Whatever it was about.'

'Shut it,' says Luke.

'Think she likes you.'

'Shut up.'

Luke tries again, after a moment. 'I could tell you loads of stories.'

'I'm reading,' Liv says, over her book.

'Things that happen while you're carwashing,' Luke says.

'My uncle lost a leg once. Car rolled over the dog, my uncle had moments to stop it, like in one of those war films –'

'Which war?' World-War-Two expert Paxman pricks up his ears.

'So he braces himself against the gatepost –'

'Please can you stop breathing egg in my face?'

'– the bonnet's up, he puts out his leg, his leg gets jammed in the engine. Then after he lost that leg, he got the other leg caught in an automatic carwash –' Luke switches scene wildly, sensing it's not going well. 'Then when he gets home he goes, what does it all mean? The meaning of life, and all that stuff?'

Liv looks at him coldly. 'Can you please go away now?'

'You don't want gory stories?'

Liv squares up to Luke. 'Which part of "go away" do you not understand?'

'Funny stories?'

'I'll make them up,' Liv says, icily.

'Trade secrets? A diamond shine without shammying off?'

'Yuk, it's a piece of animal skin.'

'What is?'

'Your shammy.'

'So're your shoes,' says Luke.

'A shammy-leather's the skin of a goat.'

'Mrs Williams says it comes from an antelope,' Luke retorts.

'Goat.'

'Antelope.'

72

'In fact the chamois is a *goat-shaped* antelope,' says Michael Paxman smoothly, in danger of death by smugness. 'Getting quite rare these days.'

'Thanks, Paxman. We didn't know that.' Geekus Maximus could get quite rare, Luke's expression says.

'Polishing cars with the skin of an endangered species,' Liv says behind her book, wondering now what she saw in 'Loony Luke's Carwash'. 'I can live without it.'

He tried to show he understood *background*. Instead, he made it worse. Luke sees in Liv's face that he got it as wrong as he could have. He forgot she went out with Matt Kramer, or he wouldn't have mentioned the garage. Unfortunate that she felt strongly about animals. If he'd known, he'd have used an old T-shirt for polishing off, instead of the skin of an antelope.

'Like all the stuff about the antelope,' says Beddoes. 'Thought you scored on that one.'

'Shut it, will you?' Luke says.

'Not sure about the uncle and the leg though. What did the dog have to do with it?'

'Leave it, all right?' Luke says.

Thanks for that, Danny. Danny grins and mouths 'nice one'. Luke could just about run over and hit him. He'd made a complete idiot out of him. The gory stories idea went down like a bucket of sick, like Danny knew it would. She didn't go for the work experience. She even had it in for shammy-leathers. Still, only the other day she'd been fascinated with the carwash. Apart from Danny winding him up, how had he got it so wrong?

When the school double-decker appears round the corner like a rusty tower-block, Luke makes a showy dive for the front of the queue to show everyone that he isn't squashed, that he doesn't give a monkey's what Liv said, and if he looked a fool, so what? Luke's posse hammer up the stairs to the top deck of the bus, throwing insults after his disappearing legs. 'Someone got egg on their face.' 'Wait a minute, Eggbreath, want to work for me?'

Liv takes a seat well away from the Lower-Sixth Goths, who occupy the left-hand side of the lower deck. Paxman sits behind her, enjoying the smell of her hair. Identifying combat planes to himself in the pages of his monthly *World At War* magazine, he turns to Dominic Wellington: 'As if he knows anything about antelopes or war films. He knows zip about war.'

'Which war?'

'Exactly.'

Dominic Wellington would like to be on friendly terms with a tall Year Eleven, even with a spoddy Year Eleven, but has never been exactly sure who Paxman is.

'What are you staring at?' Paxman says, annoyed.

Dominic Wellington eyes Michael Paxman through strong prescription glasses. 'Dad says you can wash the car, Wednesday,' he pipes up, at last.

'Luke Couch, you mean.'

'Yes.' Wellington smiles weakly. 'We got your card through the door.'

'Luke Couch washes cars, you moron, not me.' Paxman

shakes out his magazine, annoyed to be talking to a Year Eight at all. 'Do I look like a red-faced idiot with a couple of buckets?'

'Loony Luke's Carwash,' says Wellington, now fully aware that he isn't sitting next to Loony Luke. Not having lived in the village long, his eyes wander anxiously over Paxman. 'What would you call one, if you had one?'

'One what?'

'I'd call my carwash, "Dominic Wellington's Carwash" – what would you call yours?'

'Shut it, Wellington, will you?'

Paxman shows his superior knowledge of any war going by ignoring the fretful Wellington and entering the competition in his magazine. As a safe Year Eight to sit next to, Ben Dent would be less annoying. 'All right, Ben?' Paxman says. Ben Dent turns, astonished to be spoken to, even by Geekus Maximus, spoddy Michael Paxman, whose general sadness is only just compensated by his being a Year Eleven. 'All right?' Ben Dent responds, aware that his own status is only helped by his father's sponsoring the football team.

Wellington subsides, but still annoys Paxman by his presence, his sticking-out ears and his stupid mistake about the carwash. Do I look like Luke Couch? Paxman wonders – surely not. Picturing himself washing cars, Paxman toys with names and decides, if in some future existence he lost his brain and ever did wash cars, he'd call himself 'Mental Mike' and wash them so much better than Couch, he'd wipe 'Loony Luke' off the map.

'As from now, don't sit next to me any more,' Paxman tells Wellington ruthlessly, finishing him off with a rucksack in the face on dismounting from the bus, in his desire to round on someone weaker, at least, not so different from anyone else.

On the school bus home that night the situations are reversed as, by chance, Paxman finds himself sitting beside Liv Bickle, who would rather not talk to him. At almost exactly the same time as the dinosaur-like school bus hauls itself up the hill past the 'free-range' egg farm, where the chickens occasionally flutter out over a smelly, bald half-acre before being shut up again, Keith Hurst Kevs through the village in the opposite direction in his souped-up Nova with full body kit, Goodmans stereo, loud exhaust and tinted windows.

Happy to be always breaking the speed limit in a village near you, he accelerates past the sign saying 'Middlehill: Please Drive Carefully Through The Village'. Flashing past 'Kitty's Kitchen', the café on the Top Road, Hurst adjusts his bass to produce a heart-churning thwunk. On his third circuit of the area, waking up ancient villagers with the sound of his approaching sound system vibrating in their tea-cups, Hurst buzzes Kramer in a lay-by on the long road up to Cap Hill. The thought that the figure beside Kramer in the black Escort might be Liv Bickle lazily crosses Hurst's mind, but then again, didn't they split?

On his way back down through the village, Hurst meets the school bus on a bend. Putting two wheels into the hedge, he inches past and throttles away up the road, leaving the back seat of the bus abuzz over the near-miss, and enhancing his reputation as a madman.

By the time he reaches his home soon afterwards, Hurst has his version of the near-accident worked out. Wasn't his fault, was it? Bus drivers, stupid thickheads, coming round corners in the middle of the road – what me, driving too fast?

'He's got to self-destruct one day,' Paxman says from his seat on the bus moments earlier, watching Hurst's tail-pipe smoking away up the road.

'Not if he kills someone first.' Liv curls her lip, as a soon-to-be learner driver herself, deeply unimpressed.

Paxman tells Liv about the time Hurst drove into a cow, which didn't improve it, but Liv returns to her book. Her determination not to talk to him only makes Paxman more talkative. He owes this unexpected chance to chat with Liv to the absence of Michelle Piper, who usually sits next to her, at a dental appointment. Aware that he's not doing himself any favours, but unable to stop himself, he transforms into Motormouth. Beginning with an account of depleted uranium shells and their effect on troops during the Gulf War, Paxman moves smoothly on through the differences between swallows and martins. 'Long forked tail, white belly, that's a swallow. What most people think are swallows, are actually martins.'

'Mmm,' says Liv. 'Is that right?'

'And swifts, of course, they're different, again.' Paxman details the differences between swifts and swallows.

Liv hunkers down in her seat. Seems a long ride through the village. Will he ever shut up?

Paxman moves on to football injuries, the time he got a stud in his calf, when Appleton jumped on his leg –

'Sorry,' Liv says, 'but I don't like to talk after a busy day.' She brings up her book, in case he hadn't noticed. 'I like to read, instead.'

'What are you reading?' Paxman says, ready to chat about it.

'*Wuthering Heights*,' Liv says, shortly.

'What's it about?' says Paxman.

'Powerless woman with nothing to do challenges society by falling for a freak,' Liv says. 'It's melodramatic, difficult to follow, and the women in it act stupidly.'

Paxman tries to read her face. 'Oh,' he says, 'I see.'

The school bus rounds the corner and Liv manages to read a second sentence. Victorian novelists might have suffered a lot, but they didn't have Michael Paxman bleating in their ear. Heathcliff would have eaten him for breakfast. *We don't talk a lot of foolish rot around here. No more of that, if you please, sir, or I'll set the mastiff on you.*

'The hole in my leg went green, where Appleton's studs went in,' Paxman says apologetically, unable to stop the football-injury story before it's properly finished. 'I had nine stitches in casualty, and the doctor said it could've gone septic if we hadn't come in when we did, and then I'd've lost that whole bit of flesh on my leg –'

Liv turns a page noisily.

'I've got the stitches at home in a jar. See the scars now?'

Paxman waggles his calf in Liv's lap. 'They don't look that bad, do they?'

Liv shoves him off.

'Do I look like I want to know the details? Why do people keep telling me horrible things?'

Paxman looks at her. Behind them, Innit shouts: 'Obvious, innit, is what I'm saying!' Someone else shouts, 'Shut it, Dent, I won't tell you again!' The back of Paxman's seat begins to shake.

'It's like being in a zoo,' Liv weeps. 'Luke Couch tells me a load of grotesque stuff this morning, now you. Why can't people leave me alone? I thought you were different,' Liv says.

A shower of cola cans from the seats upstairs rains down into the hedges as they pass. The cola cans will sit in the hedge long after the people who threw them have left school and gone away, never remembering this last day of term.

To Paxman's surprise and embarrassment, more tears slide down Liv's face.

'I am different,' Paxman says. 'Sorry about the stitches thing, I didn't mean to upset you –'

'It's not your fault,' Liv says, cuffing away her tears. 'Don't say anything, will you, but I may not be coming back.'

'What, not to the sixth form?'

'I'm not sure. Maybe not. Don't say anything, will you?'

Paxman digests this silently, hoping his silence is helpful. Clever, cool, beautiful Liv Bickle, obviously sixth-form material, why might she not come back? Are they really not home, yet? Rain spurts on to the roof and lashes the bus windows – hard to see where they are – oh, almost in Middlehill. Paxman glances at Liv. Anything he might say now might trigger those tears in her eyes, trembling now over *Wuthering Heights*, into a fully fledged storm . . .

At last the bus shudders to a halt. Paxman feels vaguely sick.

'See, it's raining – that's how I feel,' Liv says. 'Human emotions described in terms of the landscape – "pathetic fallacy", it's called.'

Not very well up on literary theory, Paxman walks a respectful distance behind her all the way home from the bus stop. And everything *does* seem grey and sad and depressing, not at all like the last day of term, especially the drooping trees and the weeping sky, now that the usually self-contained Liv has let him into her mood.

Not everyone has the same view. 'Lucky for some!' Luke whoops, leaping off the bus and bashing Ally Carpenter's umbrella out of her hand in an excess of high spirits not meant to cause any offence.

Ally retrieves her umbrella. 'Bog off, Luke,' she says.

Luke bogs off down the road with his posse, oblivious to the rain. Running up hedges, shaking water-laden branches over one another, they go whooping down the road towards the bend at White Cottage.

Bix sees them coming round it.

Up in the tree in the hedge, the sight of a far-off but triumphant parade is heralded by a flash of Luke's school-shirt between the pub and White Cottage. Now she can hear them, Luke Couch's voice most insistent of all, Innit's basketball klaxon blaring around the bend. What a racket. You'd think they won the lottery or something. You can hear them in the valley, I bet.

And here they come, Luke in the lead, approaching slowly with many diversions for bag-fights, stuffing Paxman's books in the letter-box, chasing the Hill Farm chickens out of the road.

And when the rest of the crew appear round the bend and come rejoicing down the road in the rain, wet and glorious and wholly uncaring, the whole village knows it's breaking-up-for-summer-holidays day, if it didn't know it before.

Chapter 9

'What did you tell me to tell her the gory stuff for?' I could of killed Danny, that night.

'It was just an ordinary carwash . . .' Danny puts on a horror-film trailer voice, '. . . an ordinary village . . . until the day Luke Couch went Loony . . .'

'Hilarious,' I'm telling him. 'Thanks for the advice.'

'What did she say?'

'Thinks I'm a freak.'

'So no change there, then,' Danny goes.

'Cheers for making me look like a fool in front of Liv.'

'You did that,' he says. I'll bash him one day, I swear it.

I like being made to look like a complete div at the bus stop, especially in front of Liv Bickle. Cheers for nothing, Danny. Breaking-up day was downhill all the way after you wound me up. The thing with Liv at the bus stop was just the beginning. I got rubbish end-of-term biology marks, now there's Reports to look forward to – can't 'lose' them any more now that they post them. We came home last day of term in the rain and Naomi Griffiths' brother put his biology worms down my back. He brought them home in a jar, supposed to be for biology coursework. Beddoes bet him two quid he wouldn't eat one, so then he did, then he threw it back up in the road. Then I put the worm he threw up down Ben Dent's back, and Ben Dent ran off blubbing. Then later, the doorbell rings and it's only Ben Dent's dad, saying If Anything of This Nature Occurs Again, he'll Take a Very Dim View.

Then we had Chinese that night, and I told Dan someone might've – I didn't say *had* – put a biology worm in his chow mein, so then he went off it, and Dad said, 'Not hungry, Danny?'

'Not much,' Danny says. 'Want to swap chow meins with me?'

Dad swaps and Danny eats. Then later Dad burps and says, 'What was in that chow mein?'

Anyway, at least we broke up. That evening Dad and me load the old table and chair from the back of the barn into the car to take it up to the garage ready for the start of my carwashing business next day. **'Spring Point Carwash, prop: Loony Luke'** – 'prop' means owner, that would be me. Danny's sign looks good.

'Why is the quad covered up?' Dad goes, in the back of the barn.

'I dunno.'

'Danny cover it up?'

'Protecting it, I 'spect.' I'm out of there before he can ask me what's wrong, and I'd have to say Danny broke it.

Next day it's the first day of the holidays, and it has to be

Spring Point Garage, and the start of some major money-making.

I set up the table on the forecourt. Set up the sign against the table.

First day I'm washing a Rover and a four-by-four in the morning, plus two Mondeos before lunch. After lunch it's quiet, so the old man asks me to tidy the office. 'Matt usually does this,' he goes. 'Got a bit behind-hand. See what you can do.'

Sometime next century, maybe. Takes me an hour to sort out the MOT bookings alone. After lunch Mrs Jamieson's sister comes up and I make her a coffee and wash her VW, then after that the post van, Mr Masters's Xantia, Sara Bedwell's 106 and a clapped-out Nissan Sunny, and then it's Tuesday.

All day Tuesday we're busy. I'm handing out business cards, it's going really well, when Wednesday Matt throws me his car-keys.

'Valet the Escort, Couch, and make it a good one,' he goes.

So I clean out his Escort reeking of fags and give it the full wash 'n' wax — black cars are always the worst to shammy off — then he tells me he'll pay up later.

'I missed two customers for you,' I'm telling him, like he cares.

'Boo-hoo,' he goes, and walks off.

I only found the whole of smut-boy's life under the seats, you don't want to know, plus a photo of him and Liv on the rollercoaster at the Walton Park Experience, and it didn't make me feel great. 'You owe me six quid,' I'm telling him later.

'How'd you make that out?'

'Full wax, plus interior valet. Make it a tenner, I won't let on about the stuff I found in the pockets.'

'Do what?' Kramer stares.

'Joke,' I'm telling him.

'Funny. Pay you later,' he says, not the words he uses.

'So when were you thinking of paying me?' I'm asking him again, yesterday.

'Don't hold your breath,' he goes, taking off Paignton way in his now wicked-looking Escort. 'Going to get my tatt removed.'

He comes back and shows me his arm: 'Get that.'

'Thought you were having it removed.'

'Put an "e" on the end instead,' he goes, trying to raise a muscle to show me 'L I V' plus an 'E'.

'LIVE – what's alive?'

'Live, as in "Live Forever", you blind?' he says, going red in the face.

'It said "Liv" before.'

For a minute I think he'll hit me. 'Did you polish those showroom cars, like I told you?'

'Polish 'em yourself.'

'You want this pitch or not?'

Hard to believe a meathead like Kramer can pull Sara Bedwell, Liv Bickle and Angie Startup, though Angie did let his tyres down outside the White Hart when she found out about Amy Thewliss, latest on his list and not as fit as Liv, but impressive for a moron like Kramer.

'I'll do the showroom after I finish,' I let Mr Slavedriver know. 'That soon enough for you?'

That night I'm out in the garden, watching Danny tend a sick chicken.

'Waste of time,' I'm telling him. 'Fox'll probably get it.'

'Like Henny-Penny, you mean?' Danny says, losing his rag.

He had this other chicken, Henny-Penny he called her, after some stupid story he had when he was a kid. The sky didn't fall on her head, like it did in the story. Instead, a fox went and ate her after Danny left her out all night. Next morning there was a pile of feathers under the pine tree.

Danny went, 'She didn't stand a chance – look, she tried to fly up the tree.'

'Difficult when you're a useless flyer.'

'Someone left the hen-house door open,' he said.

'Probably you,' I told him, when Danny gets up and thumps me in the back and runs away down the road.

Mum came out, and said, 'What did you do that for?'

'What, me?' I told her. 'I never said anything.'

That was a different chicken from the one he's tending tonight, but you still can't say anything. Tonight he's in a mood cos he can't remember their names. 'Which one's this?' he goes.

'Groggy, isn't it?'

'You stay away from her,' he goes, locking the hen-house door. 'She'll roost and then she'll be fine.'

'I'm not touching her,' I'm telling him. 'Who wants to touch your scabby chickens?'

It's then that I realize Liv's over the hedge, probably reading on the bench in their garden, next door. A quick squiz through the brambles by the rusty old bog by the bank, and I'm certain it's her. Dingbat Bix is yakking to her from the tree. I sneak back to the barn and get a spade and my shammy. Then I sneak down our side of the hedge till I'm behind the place where Liv's reading. Then I start digging, throwing up soil, making a racket, singing.

Liv's head pops up over the hedge. 'Luke – what are you doing?'

'Digging a grave.'

'Making enough noise about it. You sound happy,' she says.

'I'm not, I'm sad.' I put on a sad face to show her.

'What died?'

'My sham-wah.' I hold up the car-polishing leather.

'You're burying your shammy?'

'Dead antelope, isn't it? Give it a decent burial.'

She looks at my face. 'You're not serious.'

For an answer, I drop it into the hole and start giving it 'Ashes to ashes –'

'Luke.'

'– dust to dust –'

'Luke. It's in poor taste.'

'I think I've got a mental blank about taste.'

'Yes,' Liv says, 'I think you have.'

We look at each other over the wall. I never stood up to the way she looks directly at me before, but this time I give as good as I get.

At last she cracks a smile. 'You are a fool,' she says.

'Skin of an endangered animal. Polishing cars with it can't be good – like to say a few words?' I put my hands together.

'I'd like to say,' she says, 'that I think you're a total loony.'

'Loony Luke, that's me.' I'm 'praying' over this hole with a dirty car-leather down it. 'Dust to dust, antelope to antelope –'

'Idiot,' she goes, but I've got her now, and she's laughing when she goes in. *You are a fool.* More power to me, she likes me now. I think I can get round anyone. Worth the price of a new sham-*wah*, to see that lovely smile.

So later, I'm thinking about it. And I reckon Liv likes me again, but she still must think I'm thick. So I'm nudging Danny off his bed. 'Got something I want you to do.'

Dan looks worried. 'What?'

'Write me a letter.'

'Why should I?'

'Dad saw the quad in the barn,' I go, casual as you like.

'Did he? When?'

'Don't worry, I covered for you. He doesn't know anything's wrong.'

Danny's face goes red. 'Who d'you want me to write to?'

'Liv Bickle.'

'You're having a laugh,' he goes. 'Liv Bickle's a Year Eleven –'

'Don't be stupid, not like that.'

'Like what, then?' Danny says.

I don't know like what. Except I wouldn't mind Liv knowing that I can be clever as well as funny and moody.

'I don't know, do I? She thinks I'm thick. You could change that.'

'Who cares what she thinks?' Dan gets into bed and puts on the telly.

'I'm a businessman. I care about misrepresentation.'

'Big words,' Danny goes. 'Mind you don't choke on 'em. This pillow stinks, you can have it.' He throws it at me.

I chuck it back. 'Takes you long enough to notice you're sleeping on sock-fumes.'

'You're such a child. Thanks a lot. Write your own stupid letter,' Dan says. 'Why not try Bix, she's your level.'

'Quad-quad, quad, quad, quad-quad –' I'm singing to 'God Save the Queen'. 'Quad-quad, quad, quad, quad-quad – QUAD, QUAD, QUAD, QUAD –'

'ALL RIGHT,' Danny shouts. 'Shut up now!'

'– QUAD-QUAD, QUAD-QUAD –'

'I SAID ALL RIGHT!' he screams.

Dan writes the letter that night on the computer: *Dear Liv, I'm sorry if you misunderstood me the other day –*

'Misunderstood what?'

'The gory stories stuff,' Dan says.

'Good,' I'm going. 'Continue.'

Danny continues: '*I hope you can forget the things I said so that we can start again —*'

'Use me for a story, you mean?'

'That's what you want, isn't it?'

I don't know what I want. 'Stick something clever in, can't you?'

Danny licks his lips. '*What's happened is a metaphor for —*'

'What's a metaphor?'

'Figure of speech likening two things, like, "the wheels came off it" – meaning something's gone wrong, like a car does.'

'I don't understand.'

'Liv misunderstood what you're like,' Danny says. 'Your relationship is the car, and the wheels came off it, right?'

That seems clearer. 'Right.'

'But what I'm going to say is, the misunderstanding is a metaphor for life.'

'I like the car stuff, stick with that.'

Danny sighs and goes on. 'I'll bung in an oxymoron,' he says. 'They love that, in English Lit.'

'What kind of moron?'

'A paradox.'

'Cheers, that helps a lot.'

Sometimes I think he's trying to make me feel thick. Danny's a lot cleverer than he looks. There's only eighteen months between us. Sometimes I think he got all the brains, and I got all the jokes.

When the letter's printed out it looks wicked, enough to impress anyone about to start A Level English Lit. It makes me sound as though I understand about writing, and it doesn't even mention the carwash. Not sure yet when I'll send it. Need to look really good. Keep it for an emergency. Danny won't let on that he wrote it, so long as I'm the only one, so far, who knows that *he filled up the quad with diesel instead of unleaded* and knackered the engine trying to start it.

Yes, a major blunder on Disaster-man's part, the source of all my power! Danny wakes up crying sometimes, he's so worried Dad'll find the quad before he's worked out what to do about it.

'Can you ask up the garage how much it'll cost to fix it?' he says to me, the other day.

So I get old man Kramer in a quiet moment. 'You know if you accidentally fill up a motor with diesel instead of unleaded –'

Old man Kramer grunts.

'– how much would it cost to fix it, if you did?'

'Cost you a packet,' he goes. 'Pump out your fuel tank, and clean it. Might have to strip down your ignition system and clean that out as well. You don't want to mix your fuel.'

'Bad news,' I'm telling Danny. 'Looks like it could be expensive to fix. Plus you damaged the engine.'

Danny looks frightened. 'What d'you mean?'

'You shouldn't have kept trying to start it. You've knackered the battery now.'

Danny starts to cry.

'I dunno how you managed to *do* it.' I'm only trying to help him.

'I couldn't see in the dark.' Danny sobs even more. 'You

shouldn't've told me to fill it up. I couldn't see which can was which.'

'Not me who broke the light in the barn. Diesel red, unleaded green, you must be blind,' I'm going.

'You won't tell Dad yet, will you, Luke? You won't, Luke, will you?' he goes.

Then yesterday, Dad goes, 'Don't see you riding the quad much these days.'

'I just went round the field,' Danny goes. 'Did it in under two minutes.'

Dad perks up. 'Two minutes, eh? I bet I can beat that,' he says.

'You can't,' Danny goes.

'I bet I can.'

'No,' goes Danny, 'you can't.'

Not with a broken quad. But now he's made Dad mad enough to ride it. He hasn't got a clue how to play it. What he wants to do is, make out Dad broke it himself. But Danny can't do that. He's got a reputation. *Tick-tock, your head's off. Only a matter of time,* I'm reminding him.

He keeps going out to the barn and trying to start the quad.

'You're only making it worse,' I'm warning him. 'You'd better tell Dad now.'

'Mr Kramer says he can clean it,' Dan says.

'And magically replace it for nothing.'

'I can pay him,' Danny says.

'In a parallel universe. Tell Dad after tea. After he's finished his coffee and before he has his shower.'

'I know when to tell him,' Danny says. 'I don't need you to tell me.'

'Oh, I think you do.'

'Keep your nose out,' Danny says. 'It's nothing to do with you. It's your fault for telling me to fill it up. You know I break things,' he goes.

'So now it's my fault.'

'You shouldn't have made me do it.'

'I didn't make you do it.'

'You said you'd tell Dad about the circular saw if I didn't.' Danny goes red again.

'Not my fault you rubbished the saw.'

He looks like he'll hit me again.

'Anyway, he won't find out. We'll think of something,' I'm telling him.

Meanwhile, I have Ultimate Power until she blows. And still he goes out and tries the quad, whenever Dad's working late. *Row-row-row*, the engine goes, smelling like a bonfire. *Row-row-row*, every time Dad leaves the house.

'What's that smoke in the barn?' Mum goes.

'Barbecue,' I'm telling her. 'Danny's cooking his goose.'

'What's he cooking?'

'Sausages, I 'spect.'

Row-row-row —

'Funny noise. Like a dying dog.'

'Danny's cooking for you.' I give Mum a look. Don't ask.

The quad sounds as bad as the circular saw. Both of them sound expensive.

'I wouldn't be you when Dad finds out,' I told Danny

last night before bed. 'You left it too long to tell him now. He's going to go ballistic.'

'You won't say anything, will you?'

'Mum's going to find out soon.'

'Please don't,' Danny begs.

He goes to bed white as a sheet. I'm not about to say anything while I've got Ultimate Power for a few more days, but he's only making it worse for himself. I'd help him if I could. Not my fault he's dogmeat. So it was me who asked him to fill up the quad, a cross-eyed sheep could have done it. So it's dark under the bench since he broke the light, he only had to look what he was doing. I'm always rooting around under there, sorting out my buckets.

It shouldn't have taken a genius to top up the quad with petrol. But somehow, I don't know how, the cans got muddled up.

Chapter 10

Like I said before, I've never actually felt like Sylvia Bickle. So they call me Bix at school, and they think I'm mad anyway, but obviously the Native American war-bonnet isn't a project I'd be telling everyone about.

I always felt a connection with stories about Native Americans. I read about counting coup, which means that you touch your enemy in battle to show that you came close enough to kill him. Then you can count it a coup and wear an eagle's feather, which is a lot more sensible when you think about it, than going around killing enemies. There's a lot of sensible things about Native American culture. Just the names of the different 'nations', or tribes, give you a feeling for prairies – Arapaho, Shoshone, Comanche, Crow, Seminole, Cherokee, Sioux, Apache, Navaho – and even these great-sounding names are just bad spellings for tribal names that had never been written down, before white men tried to understand them.

While Liv was going through the setting-things-on-fire-in-the-shed phase, I read *Hiawatha*. I know Native Americans would probably say it had nothing to do with their culture.

But I loved the world it made, and I lived in it for days. The saddest book I ever read was *Bury my Heart at Wounded Knee*. I don't want to talk about it.

I read about the last stand of the great leader, Cochise, in his mountain stronghold. I should have been doing school-work. I should do schoolwork now. I've got a homework programme that I'm supposed to keep up to date with, so I don't fall behind my year. I've been doing all right, so far, except I hate reporting to Mr Fowler, who's supposed to be my tutor. Maybe I'd have been called 'Sits In a Tree and Puts Things Off' if I'd been a Cherokee squaw, but who wants to be a squaw, and sit at home scraping hides?

Instead, I've been washing the swans' feathers I found in the loft cupboard. Liv said they were smelly, but you should see how white they've come up. A few soap flakes in a bucket to gently de-grease them. Rinse well, then let them dry naturally. So long as I've got a box of clean feathers, I thought I'd make a Native American war-bonnet. Strictly as an experiment, of course.

'Never mind washing feathers,' Mum says. 'You should be studying for school.'

'I'm up on it.'

'Are you?'

'*Yes.*'

Mr Fowler says I can have extra help if I go back part-time in September. You're clever, he says. You can do it. If I can't cope, I'll repeat a year. But I don't want to have to do that. It's all pressure, which makes me feel worse. I may go back part-time, I don't know. I told Mum, Depends how

I feel. It can take a long time to get over glandular fever. Longer, if you feel stressed. I have to rest in the tree every day. No use trying to rush it.

Practical projects are good for me, even Mum agrees. 'School phobia responds well to projects which encourage initiative,' she reads from this pamphlet.

'I haven't *got* school phobia.'

'Of course not,' Mum agrees.

The thing is, I'm actually quite lazy, so I haven't done any research to find out what a war-bonnet's like? I could have gone to the museum to do some research, it would have been easy to go to town with Liv, but I couldn't make myself do it. I don't like crowds. Or shopping.

Liv likes shopping a lot. She went to town the other day to get herself the chain-belt that Matt Kramer promised to get her before they broke up. When she came back she looked upset.

'What's wrong?' I asked her.

No answer.

'Liv.'

'Leave me alone, I'm all right.'

I knew she'd been to the doctor, but what about? A vaccination against Matthew Kramer, hopefully. Keep viruses at bay. Symptoms of infection by the Matthew Kramer virus include a rush to the head when the phone rings and blindness to major faults. He wrote her a letter once after they broke up: 'Plese come back, can we make it up, I will always care for you.' Then when she didn't reply, he wrote again – 'I rote to you to say how much you mean to me. Is there anything in my letter we need to discus?' Yes, she said, when she wrote back. You might want to look at the spelling.

'Did you have a hot chocolate in town?' I asked Liv.

'Actually I went to the museum.'

'Ho-hum.'

Actually she went to the museum to look at Romantic paintings of ladies in wispy outfits pining away for love. She told me they had lots of Native American artifacts in another department downstairs, but I couldn't be bothered to listen. Makes me tired to think about them. Tired, even to tell.

'Thought you liked Native American culture,' she says.

'I do.'

'So come, next time.'

'You go.'

Sometimes I get so tired I can't even make myself talk. Then I go off up the tree and look down on the world and things actually start to make sense. This morning the sun's out early, so I've spread the swans' feathers out on the grass and they're drying off really nicely. When they're dry, I'm dipping the ends of them in ink, to make them look like eagle's feathers.

The idea is to stick the feathers evenly between two long strips of leather I bought from 'Marcina's Busy Hands', this weird little sewing shop in town run by a man dressed as a woman. He usually wears a black wig and hoop earrings, sells ribbons, tape, thread, beads, knitting patterns, etc., and alters clothes, but you don't want to get caught in a conversation with Marcina, unless you have a lot of time on your hands and you can drag your eyes off her make-up, which is weird, to say the least, not to mention the outfits.

'I want one of those floor-length war-bonnets where the feathers run all the way down your back,' I told Marcina.

'I'm with you, dear,' she said. 'Will you be wanting much Velcro? How are you planning to tie it?'

I hadn't actually got that far. But with Marcina's help the project grew from a mad idea to a replica of Cochise's headdress in the only photograph taken of him, before he died defending his mountain stronghold. Marcina helped me copy the beading around those circular things at the jawline, where long feathers hang by your ears. 'Where will the party be, dear?' she said. 'Are you planning a tomahawk?'

I told Marcina, no party.

'What a shame,' she said. 'I got up a *fabulous* Roman gladiator out of cans and tinfoil last New Year.'

For years I wanted a breastplate made of quills stitched in rows, but I think I'm over that now. I know it all means something. I know I should look it up properly. I know that each eagle feather represents a 'coup', a brave deed, or a touch with an enemy, not a fashion accessory, not that women could count coup – but I just get so tired all the time.

Talking of fashion accesssories, when Liv brought home the chain-belt, I told her it was gross.

'Liv,' I said, 'it's gross.'

'Not that bad, is it?' she says.

'I thought you were getting it in silver.'

Liv loops on the chain-belt anyway. 'They only had gold ones left.'

'I can see why,' I said.

'Gross, isn't it?' Liv looks at herself in the mirror. 'I don't care, I'm wearing it anyway.'

She sits on her bed and starts to cry, so now I'm hugging her tight.

'Everything's ruined,' she says. 'Nothing planned for my birthday, no boyfriend, the wrong present – why do I even bother?'

'Because you don't need him, and you're going to wear it anyway?'

'I'm off boys for ever.' She sniffs. 'They're either horrible, pathetic or taken.'

Or all three, in Matt Kramer's case.

'I could have got you the belt before they sold out in silver,' I said. I wish I'd thought of it.

'Gold's good,' Liv sniffs. 'I'm wearing it on my birthday anyway,' she says. 'And I'm *going out to have a good time.*'

She stands and primps in the mirror, and the gold chain-belt does actually look all right on her, but Liv could wear fuse-wire and look good, she's just so amazingly beautiful. Her skin's got a lovely bloom on it, her hair gleams – she's got a kind of *glow* about her, and a bit of a belly.

She turns to one side in front of the mirror.

'Belly,' I say.

She sucks it in. 'Rubbish,' she says. 'No problem.'

She goes into her room and comes out again later in this

baggy old dress and floats away up the road. Mum's always complaining she looks like a sack. 'Why are you wearing old clothes?'

'Ever heard of Boho chic?'

'What-sheek?' Mum says.

'Bohemian – like an artist. It means wearing thrift-shop clothes.'

'You look like a walking thrift-shop,' Mum says.

'Whatever,' Liv says, coolly.

Since the holidays started she's been going up the road in strange retro clothes, sometimes in Mum's Jimi Hendrix hat, a cool black hat tied with a scarf that's been dragged through puddles at most major oldie festivals.

I'm in the tree when she comes out of the house with the baggy old flower-print dress she changed into, ballooning around her in the wind.

'Where did you get the nightdress?' I'm calling down from the tree.

'Loft cupboard!' Liv looks up. 'And it's a smock, not a nightdress!'

'Nightmare, if you ask me.'

Liv walks round to the tree and holds out her skirts. 'It's Romantic,' she says.

'Obviously – what's with the hat?'

'Writers are allowed to look eccentric.'

'Every day?'

'Writers need rituals,' she says. 'I'm writing at Kitty's Kitchen.'

'Thought you were getting a summer job!' I'm shouting

after her, as she's floating away up the road. And I still don't get the hat, even though it suits her, or the hideous, baggy clothes she's been wearing lately.

At least I can raid her cool clothes, myself. Today I'm in Liv's black spaghetti-string vest, and she's so busy being a 'writer', she hasn't noticed. People think she's stuck-up already, now they'll think she's mad. I'm stuck-up because I sit up the tree. Luke's all right, he washes cars. Paxman's sad, because he doesn't. Danny's in danger of being stuck-up, which is why he hides books when he reads them – I see him sometimes, reading at the bottom of the field.

I don't understand why you can't be clever and popular – boys because they can't be both and have mates who aren't, girls because they can't be themselves if they're clever, because round here you're meant to hide it. It's never all right for boys to be clever, unless they're making money, like Luke. Having an eye for business is an all-right sort of cleverness. Trying to be a writer isn't. It's actually a lot more complicated than that. But I think you can see what I'm getting at. I'm wondering what Liv's actually writing up at Kitty's Kitchen, when the sound of clunking buckets comes round the corner of the road.

'Here he comes. The carwash man.'

Luke clunks round the bend and stops underneath the tree. 'First cuckoo of spring – don't you get bored being nosy?'

'How's Spring Point Garage working out for you?' I can actually *see* the flat forecourt roof of Spring Point Garage, between the trees on the Top Road.

'How'd you know I'm working there?' Luke says suspiciously.

'The huge great sign outside it?'

'Good sign, isn't it?' Luke says. 'Danny done that for me.'

'So how's it going?'

'Good. Pitch up there's worth a mint.'

'Saving up for something, are we?'

Luke gives me his evil grin. 'Blow-out at Odyssey, Saturday.'

'All right for some.' For God's sake, I *sound* like him now.

He goes off whistling down the road, and I can just picture him at the Odyssey store, buying up half the place. I can so see him ordering everything in the electrical department, Gamestation Two included. What, no more stuff to show off with? You must be having a laugh.

Later, there's an upset next door – a burning smell from the barn, a whining, tearing sound, then lots of smoke and shouting.

'Luke!' His dad's yelling outside the barn. 'What did you do to this saw? LUKE, I SAID COME HERE NOW!'

Luke comes out of the back door. 'What?'

'THIS SAW, WHO USED IT LAST?'

'Calm down,' Luke says. 'Not me.'

'Someone's chewed up the saw blade – look at the state of this edge, it's completely bent out of shape. Someone's tried to use it and burned out the motor –'

'Dan,' Luke says, 'not me.'

'What did he do, stick a tree in it?'

'No,' Luke says. 'A bed.'

'DANNY GET HERE!' Mr Couch yells.

Dan comes out. 'What?'

'Did you break the circular saw?'

'I know it makes a noise,' Danny says. 'I didn't know it was broken —'

'Did you bend the saw blade out of shape?'

'It wasn't my fault,' says Danny. 'I never saw the castor until it went in —'

'You ran a *castor* under it? Do you know how much these blades *cost*?'

Danny follows Mr Couch into the barn. The sound of raised voices come out of it.

Luke's eyes meet mine through the tree, and I know that he knows that I know that Daniel Clinton Couch has some hard explaining to do, and that he, Luke, doesn't mind if he does, because it balances up with Danny the things that Loony Luke, business supremo and village entertainer, will never be able to do at all, like love a poem, sketch a tree, tend a sick chicken and know how to cover up, so that no one up at the bus stop suspects you have tender feelings taking wing inside you, just pecking, pecking, pecking, waiting until they come out.

Chapter 11

Hodge the cat shoots across the road, narrowly missed by Keith Hurst as he Kevs through the village in his Nova. The sound of Keith Hurst's exhaust drowns out Tiggy Bigglelowe's morning barking session before dying away into the distance. Other villages brace themselves, and snatch in their cats and children. Moments later, a near-miss in the valley brings Hurst nose-to-nose with Liv and her mother in their newly cleaned car.

Two weeks into the holidays. Above the village an aircraft circles, taking photographs. Later, a man with framed aerial photographs of properties in the area will call at every house collecting orders, and some people will order a Unique Portrait of Their Home From the Air, after the man explains that this lovingly framed portrait of their property will be otherwise thrown away.

Over the Paxmans' stairwell a framed aerial photograph of 'The Orchard' labelled *Masterson Photography*, *05/06/98*, hangs over the boot and shoe rack to remind Michael and his parents of another photographer, another chance to purchase a Unique Portrait, another aeroplane, another summer.

A squirrel that will never see another summer lies squashed in the road outside the Chapel. More roadkill lies on all the roads up to the Top Road, rabbits, hedgehogs, badgers, some in peculiar attitudes, making peculiar shapes that could easily be taken for objects, while objects pose as animals, leading learner-drivers to make emergency stops for a pile of dung that looks very like a hurt rabbit.

Mrs Chippy, the tabby-cat, sits washing herself in a patch of sunlight in Mrs Oliff's garden. Mrs Oliff's neighbour, Rosie Startup, knows Mrs Chippy as 'Molly', and, like Mrs Oliff, is under the impression that she owns her. Mrs Chippy leads a comfortable double life between the Startups and Mrs Oliff, who feeds and grooms and fusses her and wonders where she goes, when she disappears for hours.

Hodge watches as Mrs Chippy exercises her claws on the side of Mrs Oliff's conservatory door before she wanders back to the Startups' for dinner in a bowl saying 'Supercat'. Hodge follows her stiffly up the road, his tail underlining the words on a sign pinned to a telegraph pole:

Missing: Short-Haired Black Cat, new to area,
family distraught, please check your garage
and outhouse – Middlehill 773400

The black cat new to the area is in fact several miles away, in a cage at the vet's. A complicated series of events will take place before he is reunited with his owners, but a new kind of sign around the village has taken the initiative with lost cats and has appeared on the Boys' Brigade door lately:

Have You Lost Your Cat?
We May Have Him!
Ring Feynton 783451

Next to this sign on the Boys' Brigade door, a computer-printed photograph of a lost ginger tom stares out of its plastic wallet. Yet another poster shows a picture of Tigger. 'My Name Is Tigger. I have one white foot. Have you seen me?'

Sometimes Michael Paxman has thought about matching lost cats with their owners, but what would be in it for him? Across at The Orchard, doing odd jobs for pocket money, a quaint notion of Mr Paxman's, Michael replaces his father's newly cleaned Earth Shoes in the shoe-rack and draws his brows together over plans for a summer job. 'D'you think Luke Couch makes much money carwashing?'

'You could ask for a job at the Garden Centre,' Mrs Paxman suggests, mildly.

'He washes cars up at the garage, as well as all round the village, so he must do pretty well.'

'Garden Centre's handy,' Mrs Paxman suggests. 'You know a lot about plants.'

'Weekends and evenings, he's up the White Hart,' Paxman says, thoughtfully. 'I saw him there Tuesday night, washing a red Fiesta.'

'The White Hart?' His mother eyes Michael over the ironing. 'I thought it was Youth Club, Tuesdays.'

'Went up Hurst's place after,' Paxman chances.

'I don't like you riding with Keith Hurst.'

'Keith's all right. He's a laugh.'

'I don't care, don't you ride with Keith Hurst again.' Mrs Paxman stamps the iron on her husband's beige clothing.

'He paid Luke to wash the Nova – even Hitman Hurst.'

'Dad could drop you at the Garden Centre.' Mrs Paxman stamps the iron. 'I said you were good with plants. I spoke to Mr Venning. He said you can go and see him any time.'

'He's got a lot of regular customers, and a load of new ones. Let's see . . . his Summer Two-for-One offer expired last week –' Paxman stabs his calculator – 'so now that's three quid a car, four quid a van, so even at two cars an hour, five days a week, over six weeks –'

'Mr Venning says Peter left, and I know he'd be keen to see you –'

'– add on evenings and weekends, no competition, two pub car-parks, plus the pitch at the garage –' Paxman stabs the 'equals' tab. A fabulous figure winks back at him. 'No overheads except car-wax. Not so loony, after all. He must be raking it in.'

Around the corner and down the road the ash tree waves in the breeze, its branches empty of Bix. Sylvie Bickle has gone to town. 'Contact lenses, pants, concealer, appointment', her shopping list reads. Dr Corvet has promised Mrs Bickle a second opinion on Sylvie's glandular fever today. As Mrs Bickle has already pointed out, Sylvie has lost months of school already, but glandular fever can't be hurried, or setbacks threaten, she knows. Sylvie's shy of school, already –

Yes. The doctor knows.

Back at Middlehill, the ash leaves whisper to themselves, getting a little crisper, a little drier, as summer advances. Rising on the Top Road, a breeze blusters down through the village, helps the ash leaves talk to themselves, and ruffles the chickens in the field behind 'The Willows', next door to the whispering, but Bix-less, ash tree. Visible from the road behind his bedroom window, Luke Couch balances accounts. Starting with the profits from the carwash, the Accounts go on to list *anything to Luke's advantage*, including possible holds over Danny, and ways to turn these into cash.

Taking out a red pen, Luke removes 'Circular Saw' from the 'Credit' column, since Dad knows about it now, and it can't possibly show up under 'Profit'. Under 'Debit' Luke enters Matt Kramer's weekly demand for fifteen per cent of the carwash profit, as 'rent' at Spring Point Garage. Under 'Credit' he enters the same thing, since old man Kramer can possibly be told at some point about the amount Matt is extorting, and some of the money clawed back. Luke thinks for a moment. Then he enters 'Hand in Till – Matt Kramer' under 'Credit'. One to think about.

Still in the now healthy-looking 'Credit' column, Luke enters 'Table' beneath 'quad'. Danny scratched the dining room table *big* time the other day, he'd forgotten about it, till now. So 'Table' is a minor plus-point, like 'Chandelier' – that's a new one he forgot about – all these things balance out Debits like 'School Report', and a downturn in pocket money.

For the moment, 'quad' is still hanging on at the head of

the 'Credit' column, but for how much longer, till Dad finds out, making it instantly worthless? Luke's red pen hovers. For now, the quad's still *major* credit, up until the last minute it isn't. Danny's debt to him over keeping quiet about the quad does need to be called in soon, though . . . still time to make Danny do something *worth* keeping quiet for so long, especially since he, Luke, might cop some of the flack for not mentioning it . . .

The letter to Liv goes in 'Debit', as something Danny knows about that could possibly be a weak point. 'Letter' balances out 'Chandelier', in 'Credit', not totally Danny's fault that one, but still it'll look that way . . .

Luke Couch balances accounts, while the ash leaves whisper outside. Credit cars *washed without Matt Kramer's knowledge*, against a token number 'officially' washed, to keep down the percentage payments, and we're smiling, since muscle-head's too thick to notice . . .

Luke closes his eyes and smiles. Almost enough, almost enough, almost, almost enough . . . The tree in the hedge waves outside the window and catches the corner of his eye. No Bix. Unusual, that. Maybe she fell out and died. Luke sits up. Didn't mean that, but what would *she* know about business?

His reflection in the glass smiles back at the young businessman in the window. Any day now, maybe even next week, debit a giant splurge at the Odyssey catalogue store against profits from the carwash, and are we laughing or what? And still almost *four money-making weeks of the holidays left* . . . Apart from Liv Bickle blanking him every morning on her way out of the house, things are looking up for Luke Couch Global Enterprises.

Why *does* she ignore him, anyway? Luke snaps out of his chair. What did he do to her this time to make her walk past in a black felt hat, as though he doesn't exist? He made her laugh over the shammy-burial, but that was a while ago now. She's working up on the Top Road, somewhere – who does she think she is? And why does her blanking him bother him so much? Why should he care what Liv Bickle thinks? The answer comes back through the ash leaves outside: *Because she made me see myself differently, when she put my name in a story* . . .

She made him a part of her world by asking about the carwash, and really wanting to know what made him tick. He never expected to connect with her world. He never expected to think about Liv Bickle. The age difference alone is enough. She's only a Sixth Former next year, cool, beautiful – it would never have occurred to him to think about her. It was a question of self-esteem. You could fancy Naomi Griffiths' sister. You could even fancy Ally Carpenter. But Liv Bickle lived in the stratosphere and was never even in sight. Then she goes out with musclehead Kramer. Women, they only want looks.

Still she asked him about carwash. She made the connection between them – what sort of connection was it? Maybe it would be a good time to post Danny's letter, the letter pointing out the intellectual side of Luke Couch: '*Dear Liv, I'm sorry if you misunderstood me the other day. I hope you can forget the things I said, so that we can start again. What's happened is a good* metaphor for wheels coming off morons, etc.' – it might be a good time to send it. Was there ever a better time to look rich and clever?

Wait till Liv sees the discman, the Rolex, the sound system and, one day, the luxury motor. The young business-man in the window pictures himself flooring the accelerator in a deep purple Boxster with cream upholstery, leaving Matt Kramer eating his dust. So the car's a long way in the future. Everyone has to start somewhere.

Luke kisses his catalogue. You and me. Odyssey. Soon.

Chapter 12

Confessions Four, the Bix Tapes. I think I scared Danny Couch.

The other day he comes out of the house really early and tries to start the quad. I was actually out early myself, so I heard him trying to start it. Rrr-worr – rrr-woor – rrr-woarrr! Then lots of smoke. I think Danny Couch is in trouble. I suspect Luke has something to do with it, it'd be a surprise if he hadn't.

The quad sounds really bad. It actually sounds quite dangerous. I was glad when Dan stopped and came out of the barn. Then I would go and stand on a branch and break it, and he would look over the hedge.

He looks in the tree for a moment, goes 'Whaa–?', and falls over the chickens, running in, so I'm pretty sure he saw me. I suppose it's not every day you see someone up a tree first thing in the morning in a full American Indian war-bonnet. I may not have wanted everyone to see me, one reason I came out so early.

I think I scared him quite a lot. Five minutes later, he comes out with Luke and pushes him up to the hedge.

'Where?' says Luke, a bit annoyed.

'It's over there – in the tree –' Danny points – 'something big, like a bird.'

Luke takes one look and snorts. 'It's Sitting Bull – you blind?'

Luke would catch me halfway down the tree with the headdress round my ears. If only I'd managed to slip down before he came out. He'll never let it go now. I'll be Sitting Bull for ever.

I'm actually really pleased with the way the war-bonnet's turned out? The weight of all those feathers on your head makes you move with more dignity, so you feel sort of *noble*, somehow. Sixty-four feathers, round my head and down my back. Sixty-four brave things I might have done. Sixty-*three* things I haven't, except for standing up to Michael Paxman the other day when he asked me, 'How much d'you think Luke makes washing cars?'

'How do I know?'

'You see everything up there, don't you?'

'He washes about ten cars a week around here.'

'That all?'

'Plus the ones I don't see. Work it out for yourself.'

He looks up at me under his bowl haircut. 'Think you're clever, don't you?'

'Yes, I'm always saying how clever I am.'

'Everyone thinks you're mad.'

'Like *you're* not Geekus Maximus.'

'Goes double for you,' he says. And off he goes over the road.

'Geekus Maximus' was cruel, but he bores people to death without mercy, so maybe it's time he should know. As spoddy as he is, he thinks he can criticize me? Maybe it was the war-bonnet that gave me the courage to say it, though I wasn't wearing it at the time. When I left it upstairs after trying it on, Dad thought I'd brought in a swan.

Now I'm really tired, probably because I got up too early. I get up early because I can't sleep. I can't sleep because I nap during the day, or I sit in the tree, and people and things pass beneath me like a dream, and don't seem entirely real. Paxman thinks that I think I'm clever, but he's wrong.

I may not be brave or wild, beautiful, Romantic or popular, or cleverer than anyone else. But Paxman's right about one thing. I do actually see everything.

Chapter 13

Luke Couch – not only making a mint, but chatting up Liv Bickle at the bus stop, like he has a chance with a Year Eleven. There's something going on, but what interest could the lovely Liv have in a prankster like Luke Couch? Whereas *he*, Michael Paxman, if not in her league, is at least in the same *year* as Liv.

Paxman broods in his room, trying to fit the pieces together. Luscious Liv, Kramer-ex, almost two years older than Couch – watching him wash her mother's car so intently that he, Michael Paxman, walks past and she doesn't even notice he exists. Then Luke offers her a job at the bus stop, what is *that* about? She gives him the elbow, but then, so what? At least she knows Luke exists.

Whereas, Paxman thinks, when did she last speak to *me*? As if he doesn't remember that never-to-be-forgotten bus ride home on the last day of term. Who sat next to Liv when she let out the secret that she might not come back to school, the only one to see tears in her eyes, *the one she confided in*? Kramer's history, apparently. No one's seen him with Liv for at least the last couple of months. Now Luke's taking up Liv's attention, somehow – what could be in it for him?

But I know things Luke doesn't, Paxman remembers. Liv confided in *me*. Move over, carwash man. You think you know everything, think again. Who do you think you are?

Danny lent him *Under Siege* and *Def Com Two* and told him all about it. Putting worms in people's chow mein. Laughing when people's chickens get eaten by foxes. Making people feel stupid whenever they break things. Posting people's books in the postbox, so that they have to hang around till the four o'clock collection to get them back. Hosing people's gardens, flattening people's dads' plants. Chatting up a Year Eleven, when they're only a manky Year Nine. Making everyone like them, with their 'funny' business cards. Paxman punches his duvet. Take that, carwash man.

Later Paxman dons his football strip, the gift of Ben Dent's dad. Ben Dent's house is spacious and cool, his freezer freighted with pizza and beer, his parents nearly always absent, so let the games begin.

Michael Paxman tells his mother that he goes to Youth Club on a Tuesday night, when in fact he goes to Ben Dent's. He used to go to Keith Hurst's, but the food is unlimited at Dent's, *and* he has a snooker room. Paxman connects with the mixed group that meets at Ben Dent's house via his shared interest in war films with Danny Couch, who is in Dent's year. Ben Dent lets Hurst and Paxman into his spacious kitchen on a Tuesday night to drink the beer in his parents' fridge and fill out his social group, despite the fact that Hurst is a chancer and Paxman's Geekus Maximus for knowing the Latin names of birds . . .

Not exactly thrilled by hanging out with Year Eights, even though he doesn't advertise the fact, 'Sad Man' Paxman looks at himself in the mirror and sees himself through Liv's eyes. Those curtains of hair, either side of his face – not only annoying, but deeply uncool – how has he worn them so long?

It's as though the scales of sadness have fallen from his eyes at last. Paxman reaches for the phone book and dials 'Barnets' where Ben, Hurst – everybody – goes to get the skinhead look. 'Hullo – is that the hairdresser?'

'Barnets men's and women's hairdressing?' a bored voice advises him.

'Are you the hairdresser next to that sewing shop – Marcina's Busy . . .'

'Hands. Were you wanting a haircut?'

'Um, yes,' Paxman says, amazed by his own decisiveness. 'Can you do me a grade one next week?'

So his mother won't like it, so what. No one cares what you know. They only care what you look like.

'Tuesday, ten-thirty, all right?' the bored voice checks.

'Fine. The name's Paxman. All right.'

Paxman rings off and feels changed. Clever equals stupid. Interesting facts are irrelevant. Which group you're in, is what matters. The Dent group includes the notorious Nash brothers, and oddballs like Danny Couch. Obviously it's Ben Dent's snooker room which is the attraction, and they'll get bored soon and move on, but why should small, squeaky Ben Dent care, if they come round on Tuesday nights and lend him a bit of glamour?

The Dent group is mixed, but hard, marginally better than belonging to a geekus Year Eleven group in the low-status seats in the common room. Being in the group is what matters. Paxman feels like getting out the scissors. What was he, blind? The bowl haircut has to go now. How can he wait until Tuesday?

So what if it upsets his mother? She has to be upset some-time, doesn't she, might as well be now. So she wants him to work at the Garden Centre, doesn't mean he's going to do it. Paxman feels something like anger rising inside his chest. Fitting in is important, can't they see? The bowl is holding him back. How long has it taken him to see it?

His curtains of hair hadn't annoyed him before he'd looked up the tree, and Sylvie 'Bix' Bickle had called him 'Geekus Maximus'. It was as though she'd dropped some-thing on him, like a cool, fresh egg of self-knowledge. It was as if he'd noticed his hair for the first time, as if he'd noticed himself . . .

He'd come home and noticed his magazines.

'You're not throwing those away?' his dad said.

Michael paused by the bins. 'Why not?'

'Series three of World at War?' Mr Paxman looked out-raged. 'Why?'

'No one reads war magazines.'

'But,' frothed Mr Paxman, 'what's wrong with having a hobby?'

'No one has hobbies, Dad.'

'Well, maybe they ought.'

'I don't want a hobby, all right?' Hobby – a spare-time occupation done for pleasure. I WANT A LAUGH LIKE EVERYONE ELSE – PLEASE CAN YOU LEAVE ME ALONE?

'No need to be rude, Michael,' his father had said, offended.

But there *is*, Paxman had thought, watching his father shift magazines laboriously from the bins to the shed. Rude's what I want to be, Dad. Rude as Hurst. Rich as Ben. Popular as – *Luke Couch.*

'Want a hand?' he offered.

'No, thank you, Michael,' his father had said. 'I'm not quite senile yet. I think I can manage without you.'

That had been just a couple of days ago. Now the desire to be *included* beats in Paxman's brain like a military tattoo. In football strip, except for the bowl, he could be just about anyone. *Blending in* is the way to go. Wait till Liv sees the new image. If he ever gets to sit next to her again on the bus, he'll try not to talk so much. He hadn't meant to, the last time. Those tears, spilling down over her chin . . . had that idiot, Luke, upset her? And if he had, then what?

Paxman puts on his football boots. Strikes a pose in the mirror. Looking good as Luke Couch, any day. What could wipe the smile off his face? What did Couch care about most, if he cared about anything at all?

In the pocket of his football shorts, Paxman finds a small, square card. **Loony Luke's Carwash. Mad Summer Rates From Cool Hand Luke, Ring Middlehill** – whatever.

Paxman crumples the card into a small, hard bullet and throws it at the wall. Brilliant. Of course. Hit him where it hurts. Paxman hammers a football against the wall. Hit him – where it – hurts –

'Michael, what are you doing?' his mother calls up the stairs.

'Studying.'

'It doesn't sound like studying.'

'I'm sorting my books out, all right?'

'Not kicking a ball against the wall?'

Paxman hammers the ball against the wall. 'Sorting – books I – told you –'

If Liv could see him now. Immaculate ball skills, massive mid-field potential. Liv and Luke Couch, are you kidding me? What would they have to talk about, fart jokes on the bus? He pictures sitting next to Liv on the school bus again, only this time she's laughing, not crying, her hair is splayed on his shoulder, her knee beside his, her leg burning against the side of his leg, for the whole of its length . . . Liv, looking at him appreciatively with those cool, direct, brown eyes. Going to town with Liv . . . eating pizza with Liv . . . riding the bus home from town, joking, hugging, kissing . . . and Couch, he would be nowhere, pushing no one around –

Bam! Bam! Bam! He smacks the ball against the wall . . .

'A little consideration, Michael, please!' his father shouts up the stairs. 'Football outside, if you don't mind!'

Nutting the ball into a corner, Paxman sweeps a death-ray around his room, until now, the room of a geekus. So much for hobbies. He guns a row of model planes off their shelf and into a carrier bag. *Ack! Ack! Ack!* Die, special-interest Sad Man!

Adding *Pears Encyclopaedia* and *Birds of Britain* to the bin, he tops them with *Heart of Darkness* and *The Making of Apocalypse Now*. So long, spod-brain. Hullo, playing Gamestation for hours and slobbing in front of the telly. How could he have been so old for so long? Feels like he's just woken up. Liv and Luke Couch, are you kidding? He, on the other hand, Michael Paxman – tall, dark and soon to be not-so-different – why wouldn't she talk to *him*?

Chapter 14

So Matty-boy throws me some keys. 'Luke, clean the Fiat, will you?'

'Clean it yourself,' I'm going.

We're standing by the till when the pumps are quiet. Nothing but sale cars outside, including a red Fiat that Matt 'dosser' Kramer's supposed to have valeted.

'I'm afraid it's the *wrong answer*,' he goes. 'You *did* have eighty-five per cent of your earnings. I'm afraid you just lost five per cent.'

He isn't afraid, at all.

'What, I'm paying you twenty per cent now? Get lost, Kramer.'

'You want the pitch, cough up.' Matt the rat dips a hand in the till and takes out as much as he wants.

'*Mister* Kramer might have something to say about that.'

'About what?' he goes, slamming the till shut and pocketing the dosh.

About *you* charging twenty per cent for the carwashing concession, I was going to say, but instead I come out with: 'Meant to take cash from the till, are we?'

'My wages,' he goes. 'Like it's your business.'

'You entered it on the till-roll then.'

'I don't have to,' he goes. 'I part own this business, all right? Twenty per cent,' he goes. 'Payable Friday, all right?'

'I'll check with Mister Kramer, shall I?' Playing my joker now. 'I only paid ten per cent last year.'

Kramer the framer plays his ace. 'You say a word to my dad, I'll tell him you robbed the till.'

What's the point? If rat-boy can rob his own dad, he can make out it was me who did it.

'Whatever,' I'm going, eventually. 'Don't throw all your teddies out of the pram.'

'*And* you can valet the Fiat before I get back from town.'

'Whatever,' I'm going. Thickhead. What does he think, I'm going to tell him how much I make, and pay him twenty per cent of it? It's not like he's going to check. He's never here, for a start. Meanwhile, the old man doesn't know, and I'm not going to tell him, that Matt pays himself from the till. Anything for a quiet life. So I'm cleaning the Fiat anyway, when Liv goes by in a hat.

She goes by in a hat most mornings, but this time she's not going to 'Kitty's Kitchen' with a bag with books sticking out of it. Instead she goes into the newsagent, and doesn't ever come out . . .

'Something on your mind?' Old man Kramer creeps up on me. He does that, sometimes. 'What's so interesting? Accident up the road?'

He squints up the road where I'm looking, just as Liv

pops out of the newsagent and puts out an ice-cream sign. 'Livvy Bickle – pretty, in't she?'

'Yes,' I'm going, 'she is.'

'Pity she don't come round here no more. Nice smile like that, round the place.'

'No,' I'm going. 'Yes.'

Then he squints round the sale cars. 'Missing customers, Luke? I thought Matt was valeting these.'

'Said I'd do it for him.'

'Oh,' the old man goes, 'why's that?'

'Said he was going out.'

The old man hisses between his teeth. 'I paid him to do it,' he goes. 'He's in for a cut in wages, he is – when is he getting back?'

'He didn't say.'

'Leave it, Luke,' the old man goes. Then he goes off and does stock-taking.

The carwash picks up later. A Merc, a Saab, then a Yaris. The Yaris takes me ten minutes, top. The bloke in the Merc gives me a two quid tip. Lunchtime, I'm off up the newsagent's for crisps, even though we stock 'em ourselves.

I go in, and there she is. 'Hi.'

'Luke – hullo.'

'Been working here long?' I'm acting surprised. 'Packet of Worcester-sauce flavour Wiggles – thanks.'

'My third day,' Liv says, handing over the Wiggles and forking out my change.

'Nice ring.'

'Matt gave it to me.' She takes it off. 'Can you give it back to him for me?'

'I suppose.'

'It's awkward – thanks.'

I have to take the ring when she gives it to me. I can't think of anything else to say. No one else in the newsagent, and Liv's not helping me out here. 'I see you go past in the morning.'

'You're down at the garage,' she says.

'Right.'

Liv stacks newspapers. She seems kind of cold and quiet.

'How'd you get the job?'

'I came in to buy a biro, saw a notice on the door, started Monday,' she goes.

'And you *were* at the café?'

'Writing,' she says, 'not working.'

I'm well confused, but that's normal with Liv. 'Nice one.'

'I suppose,' she says, like she's going to cry.

'Least you're earning.'

'Yes,' she says, 'I'm earning. So how's it going with Matt?'

'Nothing I can't handle.' Then I tell her. 'He went out with Thewliss last week.'

'Kim Thewliss?'

'Amy. Bowling, Thursday. White Hart, Wednesday night.'

'I thought I saw him with someone,' she says. 'I didn't know it was Amy.'

'You're better off, if you ask me.'

'Anything else?' Liv says.

'He's a pain to work with.'

'I mean,' says Liv, 'anything else I can get you?'

'No, ta – fancy a Wiggle?'

'Think I'll pass,' Liv says, going green with the whiff of Worcester sauce, when I open them up and waft 'em. Anything else I can get you, she says. How about some eye contact to tell me you know I'm human? 'Better get going.'

She doesn't look up.

'Well, I'm off, now – thanks.'

Take care, Luke, I'm going to myself outside, because Liv isn't about to say it. Look after yourself. Don't work too hard at the garage with Matt. But maybe Matt's the problem. You could understand why, if you didn't know him. When you know him, you think, what?

Rat-boy comes back from town long enough to change into the clothes he just bought. 'Like it?' he goes.

'Nice.' If you like townie jumpers and chatty leather jackets.

He nicks off again quickly, before the old man looks up from his sandwiches in the office. 'Later, Couch.'

'Can't wait.'

The rest of the lunch-hour's grim, thanks to Mr Top Man piking off in his Escort to hang with Thewliss at the Cricket Club. Meanwhile, it's down to me to mind the shop and the till and wash a van and a hatchback.

So I'm miles away while I'm hosing down this Fiesta, thinking, why does he get to pike off? Why is it always people like Kramer who get to go out with Liv, have family businesses ready to step into, flash cars, everything they want –

'Top up my tyres?' says Fiesta bloke.

'Oh,' I'm saying. 'Right.'

– why should a waste of space like Kramer have everything going for him, I'm thinking, while I'm topping up this bloke's tyres – when people who put in the work get to sweep the floor in front of him, and nothing ever puts a dent in his bodywork and he goes on getting lucky –

'Wake up, boyo, you'll blow 'em out!' Fiesta man snatches the air hose.

'Sorry?' I'm going. 'What happened?'

'Wake up and look at the gauge,' he goes. 'Fifty pounds pressure per square inch, when they should be at thirty-two! I'm not Jensen Button,' he goes. 'I don't need racing tyres to pick up a pasty in Alfington.'

I blew up his tyres so hard, they almost exploded! 'Sorry, I wasn't thinking!'

Fiesta man lets out some air and drives away in a mood.

'I think you was thinking too much,' says old man Kramer. 'Got a bee in your bonnet, or something?'

Doesn't stop me thinking all afternoon. Kramer, Liv, Bix – did I mention mad girl Bix scared Danny the other day? He drags me out of bed in a panic. 'There's something stuck in the tree,' he goes. 'Something big, like a bird.'

We go outside, and she's only up the tree in a Red Indian get-up. 'What are you, blind?' I'm going. 'It's *her*.'

'Bix?'

'No, a giant bird, you div.' I'm annoyed he got me out of bed for Sitting Bull. 'Why are you out here so early?'

'Dad's taking the quad down the sewage farm,' Danny goes. 'He bet me three hot dogs he'd do it in under three minutes.'

'Tonight?' I'm going.

'Yes,' Danny goes. 'I came out to try to start it, but –'

'Smoke?' I'm going.

'Right,' Danny goes. 'What am I going to do?'

'Who knows?' I'm going. 'I'm so glad I'm not you.'

We're watching the dingbat climb down the tree next door with a big pile of feathers on her head, when Danny starts to sniffle. 'I don't care,' he goes. 'I can't stand it, any more. I'll be glad when it's over.'

You say that now, I'm thinking. 'You should've said something before.'

'I couldn't, after the circular saw.'

Danny sweats for hours, but Dad works late that night. The bet's still on, that's the trouble. Dad doesn't forget things like that. Danny forgets a lot of things. Last night I remembered I told him to post my letter.

'Did you post that letter for me, or what?' I'm thinking he might have forgotten it.

'What letter?' Surprises, he has.

'The letter to Liv.'

'I'll do it tomorrow,' he goes.

'You better,' I'm reminding him, 'or Dad's going to remember that bet.'

'Don't care if he does.'

'I think you do.'

I give it three days, top. Till the weekend, in fact, before Dad tries to start up the quad. Still Danny thinks he can put it off. Like the world's going to change or something.

'I can save up and mend it,' he goes.

'In dream-world,' I'm going. 'You're dogmeat.'

Danny doesn't have that kind of money. There again, I do . . . Carwashing gives you time to think, as well as making you rich. So I'm hosing off a Mondeo, making more money without even trying, when Kramer pulls up on the forecourt, with Keith Hurst's Nova behind him. He and 'Hitman' Hurst climb out of their motors together like Dumb and Dumber, special offer village idiots, Two For the Price of One.

'Back from the Cricket Club already?' I'm letting Kramer know we all noticed how long he's been gone.

'Cleaned the Fiat yet, Couch?' Kramer goes, ignoring me and trying to impress Hurst. 'Time is money, remember?'

'Mister Kramer told me to leave it. He told me *you* had to do it.'

'As if.' Kramer laughs, but he's worried. 'Loony Luke's no-wash tomorrow, unless *all the sale cars on the forecourt* get the once-over, all right?'

He pushes over my sign with his foot, so I switch direction with the hose accidentally-on-purpose and give him a dose.

'Turn it off!' Kramer squawks. 'For God's sake, you stupid –'

'Liv sent you this.' I throw down her ring in a puddle. 'Don't give it to Amy Thewliss.'

'My sister had a ring like this.' The Hitman picks it up. 'You didn't sleep with her, did you?'

'What are you talking about?' Kramer says. 'Congratulations, Couch, you ruined my shoes.'

'Your dad says he'll cut your wages.' I'm thinking he should know.

'When did he say that?' Kramer moves away from Hurst.

'After you piked off this morning.'

'Poor Lukey,' Hurst yuks. 'Left you to it, did he? Loony Luke's Slavey Shop. Luke's White-wash and Please-Don't-Hurt-Me Very Quiet Waxing Service.'

'Shut it, Keith,' Kramer goes.

Hurst gets into his car and revs up. 'I better not find out this ring belonged to my sister.'

The old man comes out of the workshop, wiping his hands on a rag. 'Good day, Luke?'

'Last one,' I'm telling him. 'Can you turn off the hose at the tap?'

'Matthew,' he says, 'you turned up, at last – bring the tractor round, will you?'

'I've got good clothes on,' Kramer says, catching the keys.

The old man looks at him. 'Don't strain yourself – Luke?'

'I'm not allowed to drive.'

'It's off-road – Matthew, please?'

'I'm not your slave.' Love-rat throws the keys at me. 'Couch can do it, can't he?'

*

After I bring the tractor round, and Fly the sheepdog jumps in, he tells me we've got sheep to look at. So we rattle off to look at his sheep.

'I didn't know you had sheep as well as the garage,' I'm saying to old man Kramer, as we rattle off in the tractor.

'I've got a few fingers in a few different pies – like you,' he says, and winks.

'I've only got the carwash.'

'Give it time. You got the touch,' he says.

We come back by Moorland Motorbikes & Accessories, which the old man owns as well. He gasses with Graham and Trevor, and we both have a cup of tea. By the time we get back to the garage, Matt's smoked a pack of twenty. 'Where were you?' he moans. 'I've been doing the shop and the pumps on my own. You missed three carwashes, Couch.'

'More where they came from.' Not my fault he missed out on the ride on the tractor. 'I'm off home now, all right?'

It's a straight walk down from the Top Road to Middlehill.

'I gave him the ring,' I say to her. I meet Liv on the way home, walking along like she's in a dream, as usual. We turn down the lane together. She even takes one of my buckets.

'Oh,' she says. 'Is that right?'

'Why were you blanking me earlier?' I'm asking her, with no one around to hear.

'When?'

'Every day, on my way to the garage?'

'I never even saw you. I'm blanking life,' Liv says.

We go on a bit. She's in a strange mood. I'm not even sure what she means. The lane's really steep past Mount Pleasant, then it goes narrow, all the way down to The Terrace, so we bump buckets as we go. 'You still want background?' I'm asking her, halfway down the lane.

'For stories, you mean?'

'Cos there's stuff going down at the carwash —'

'I can't care about that now.'

Did she get my letter yet, or what? Our buckets bump, it's embarrassing, so I let her go ahead. When the path opens out again, she says, 'I got my GCSE results.'

'What were they like?'

'Pretty good.'

'How many A's?'

'You don't want to know.'

'You're clever.' She is. 'I do.'

She glances at me and goes a bit red. 'Five A stars, three A's and two B's.'

'That's brilliant — wish I could do that.'

'You don't have to.'

'No.' She looks at me, and she knows what I'm like. 'Good job, cos I haven't got a clue.'

'That's not true.'

'It is though.'

'No,' she's going, 'it isn't.'

'If you could have anything, what would you want?' I'm asking her down by the Donkey Park, with no one around to hear, just donkeys tearing grass on the other side of the wall.

'I'd want Matt to come to my birthday,' she says, 'even though we broke up.'

She looks at me sadly.

'For real?'

She nods and swaps buckets with me, so I get the broken handle, and I know she let me into a secret. Maybe she got my letter. *I hope you can forget what I said. So we can start again.*

'What would you want,' she says, 'if you could have anything?'

'Everything in the Odyssey catalogue with a plug on it?'

Liv laughs. 'Really?'

'Why not?'

'Don't always get what you want,' she goes. 'For your sake, I hope you don't.'

We're passing the Turpitzs' place, when Innit *would* be sitting on the wall. 'Yo – what are you doing?'

'Walking home, what does it look like?'

'Been carwashing? – Hi, Liv,' he goes.

Liv says 'Hi' and walks on.

'Bit crap, innit?' he says.

'What is?'

'The holidays.'

'Not if you're earning,' I'm saying.

'All right for some, innit?' he goes.

'What d'you mean?'

'Liv Bickle.'

'Don't be stupid.'

I catch her up by the signpost. *Middlehill. Please Drive Carefully.*

'Does he think you're in with a chance then?' she says. She looks at me. 'Well?' she goes. She's laughing at me now.

'Don't hold back,' I'm going. 'Say what you really think.'

'He asked you about me, didn't he?'

'As if.' I'm laughing at her now, the way she just comes out and says it. 'Innit, he's such a div.'

We swing round the bend by White Cottage. On the corner by the Boys' Brigade hut, we stop and I take back the bucket. 'Cheers, then. Thanks for carrying it.'

It's like the mood's over or something. We really don't want to be coming round the corner together, not with Beddoes' house near. Liv doesn't need the grief. Goes double for me, with that hat.

'Thanks for today,' she says. 'The ring, I mean – everything.'

'Forget it. No problemo.'

'Bye now,' she says. Then she comes back. 'You should drop the "loony" act more often. You're all right, Luke,' she says.

I'm going, 'I'm normal, me.'

'Sorry about Sylvie,' she goes.

'The feathers thing, up the tree?'

'She gets a bit bored sometimes.'

'She isn't like you,' I'm saying.

'No,' Liv says. 'She's different. She likes to be different,' Liv says.

Different and mad, I'm thinking.

When I get in, I lie down. I think Liv and I may be friends. I never had a friend like her before. Something changed since the carwash. Since Liv and the carwash, I mean. This summer Loony Luke went mature.

I may even stop winding Danny up – then again, why bother?

Chapter 15

Bit crap, innit, Innit would say. But holidays aren't crap if you're earning. And Chris 'Innit' Turpitz isn't in the Odyssey catalogue store, with a ton or more to spend . . .

Luke Couch, young businessman and potential big spender, hugs these thoughts to himself as he fills in an order form, pays at the till, and finds his way to the waiting area labelled 'Chairs'.

'Order number *six hundred and seventy-four*, to your Collection Point, please.'

The heat and bustle of the crowd under the lights makes children cry and old people faint. Everywhere goods are on display. Under the jewellery counter rings revolve slowly in velvet rollers, like hot-dog sausages at the cinema. 'Silver' necklaces with dodgy hallmarks fill the stand on top, everything very glittery, very cheap, very Odyssey.

'Order number *six hundred and seventy-nine*, to your Collection Point, please.'

A tired-looking man with a child moves to Collection Point B.

'The numbers never come up in the right order, do

they?' sighs a woman beside Luke. 'I've got six hundred and seventy-five.'

Luke shows her his ticket – six hundred and seventy.

'You'd think they'd do them in order,' complains his neighbour. 'Suppose they'll do the earlier ones soon.'

Luke shrugs. 'Suppose. I don't know.'

In fact he knows very well the odd way the numbers come up. Here to collect the fruits of many weeks' labour on the carwash, his ticket clutched in his sweaty little hand, he knows to a 'T' when each of them is liable to pop up onscreen overhead, when his order number will be announced over the annoying tannoy.

Meanwhile, the heat, light and noise increase until children tumble out of the edge of the crowd and soft toys are trampled underfoot. A stand full of steam irons interrupts the flow of shoppers entering the already-full store.

'Hell in here, isn't it?' the woman next to Luke says. 'I can't stand the stress at my age.'

'I'm fourteen and I can't,' says Luke, wishing it would soon be over.

On display in the window is an exhausted family, who have collapsed into a cream leather three-piece suite labelled PAY NOTHING NOW!!!

Behind the suite, stands filled with picnic baskets, robot dogs, cutlery sets, hoovers, dolls, towels, garden tools and catalogues make a maze across the floor. A woman pushing a pushchair with a crying child inside it heads for an empty chair and misses it by seconds. Luke jumps up. 'Here you go.'

'Thanks a lot.' The woman subsides into his chair.

Over in Exchange And Refund an argument rages over the return of a mobile phone without its packaging. 'We have to have *everything*,' the assistant insists. 'The phone, the packaging, and the charger.'

'Order number *six hundred and seventy*, to your Collection Point, please.'

'Lucky you,' Luke's neighbour says. 'That's you, isn't it?'

Luke crosses to join the queue at Collection Point D. While waiting, he checks out the display on the industrial shelving units which receive the goods tumbling down the chutes behind the counter – breadbins, torches, radios, novelty mobile phones. SPREAD THE COST WITH AN ODYSSEY CARD announces an orange sign.

'Six-seven-oh?' an assistant enquires, reading the number on a box.

Luke steps forward and hands her his ticket.

After much checking of the ticket listing his purchases against variously sized boxes, Luke receives a jumbo turquoise carrier bag and emerges from the queue at last.

'Order number *six hundred and seventy-five*, to your Collection Point, please.'

Luke catches her eye as his neighbour in Chairs rises to collect a Foot Spa, unaware that she'll be back next week in Exchange And Refund, after its Three Setting Modes break down.

Clutching his bag, part of Odyssey, and hating Odyssey, Luke makes good his escape.

*

Outside at last, the heat of shopping fever and the grizzle of small children behind him, a feeling of satisfaction washes over Luke Couch. The carrier bag of electrical goods is what he's worked and slaved for, put up with Kramer for, got dirty and hot and annoyed for. Holidays might be rubbish if you're Innit, and unemployed. If you're earning, they're an enrichment opportunity. Earning is what it's about.

Declining his mates' invitation to spend a small fortune at the bowling alley and damage a burger or two, Luke hugs his jumbo Odyssey bag all the way home on the bus. At the bus stop he whips out his mobile and calls his mother at home. 'It's me . . . the bus stop in Alfington . . . can you come and get me?'

Some ten minutes later, a Volvo pulls up.

'Got what you wanted then?' Mrs Couch asks vaguely, as Luke bundles his bag into the back.

'They didn't have the DVD player,' Luke says. 'Got everything else, 'cept the CD rack.'

'You'd better check that everything works,' Mrs Couch advises. 'That Odyssey stuff's always rubbish.'

Luke ticks off the price of his purchases all the way down through the lanes. Passing the end of Raggin Lane, a lurid sign catches his eye –

'Stop a minute – *what?*'

Mrs Couch stops at the junction.

'Back up a minute,' says Luke. 'I don't believe it – see that?'

'MENTAL MIKE'S MOBILE CARWASH', the sign outside Paxman's house announces. 'Mobile Car Cleaning

Service, Ten Mile Radius, All Major Credit Cards Accepted.'

'"Mental Mike", he's having a laugh. He can't just copy me, can he?' Luke squeaks. 'How can he be *mobile*?'

Mrs Couch shrugs. 'Maybe his dad helps him out.'

'Yeah, but he'll nick all my business.'

'Not,' says Mrs Couch, 'if you do a better job than he does.'

'A squirrel could do a better job than Paxman.'

'Nothing to worry about then, is there?'

'Mental Mike' – what a rip-off of Loony Luke, the original and *best*. Even when the Odyssey bag has spilled its contents over Luke's bed in a reassuring jumble of packages, he feels like marching over the road and ripping down Paxman's sign.

But nothing takes the shine off the Gamestation Two with Rumblepack As Standard. Eat carwax, Paxman. Be a long time before you earn *this*. Gloating almost audibly, Luke unpacks the console and loads a CD.

Or tries to.

When the screen reads 'Game Loaded', it isn't. Not a sausage comes up on-screen. Luke calls the helpline. Waits forty minutes. Gets a repeated message: *Problems with Gamestation Two mean that some editions won't load. Please contact your retailer. Problems with Gamestation Two –*

The video recorder clunks too, so noisily that it won't rewind – also Video Plus won't kick in. The sports watch he bought has a nasty scratch across its dial, and the telly's missing an aerial – and the camera with Lo-Cost Zoom has a badly battered case, and the wind-on feels iffy. Luke's heart sinks. Looks like a trip to Exchange And Refund. Why doesn't *anything* live up to what you think it's going to be, not even things you worked for?

Something he spots out of the window makes him feel even worse.

As if he'd ever known when it was, now it feels like he's known, and forgotten. A sheet over the sign at the junction says, 'LIV – SIXTEEN TODAY!'

He didn't know it was her birthday.

He'd have sent her a card, if he'd known. Luke feels a tug at his heart. If he'd ever felt it before, he'd have recognized it as – what?

Chapter 16

Confessions Five, the Bix Tapes. Me and Dad raided the airing cupboard last night. Then we put up old bed sheets all round the village, saying LIV – SWEET SIXTEEN all over them!

I'd threatened to do it once, after Naomi Griffith's sister put up a sheet saying *Naomi, Eighteen At Last!* on the Alfington roundabout, a few months ago. I'll do that for you when you're sixteen, I said. Liv said, You're dead, if you do.

She thought I'd forgotten. Liv's watching telly last night with no idea we'd remember to embarrass her all over the village for her birthday next day, but Dad winks at me after tea, and I slip out for magic markers. Liv's staying in. She won't see them until her birthday tomorrow morning, so his wink says, 'Let's put up the sheets.'

I mean, it's traditional, isn't it, like loot bags at parties when you're a kid, and taking home birthday cake in cling film and throwing it away.

We used red marker pen in the end, and cut the sheets into four. We hung the biggest sign over the junction opposite our house. Then we drove up through the village and hung one by the Garden Centre saying LIV – HAPPY 16th!

Dad suggested putting one over the sign for 'Middlehill' on the Top Road, but I thought that that was an uncharacteristically dangerous suggestion. 'Won't it distract drivers? What about people looking for Middlehill?'

'No one *looks* for Middlehill,' Dad says. 'You live there, or you don't need to know.'

We drove back down through the village and hung a sign outside The White Hart and one by the village hall. That was all our signs, and I reckoned they were embarrassing enough . . .

Happy birthday, Liv. She goes to bed looking sad, and doesn't say 'goodnight'.

This morning Liv gets up and, after I point her to the window, she blushes to the roots of her hair. LIV – SWEET SIXTEEN says the sign at the junction, in bright-red marker pen. 'Oh, what,' she says, 'you put *signs* up?'

'And how.'

'My *name's* all over the village?'

'Obviously,' I'm saying. 'Think we'd let your birthday go by without the traditional embarrassment of signs everywhere?'

'I can't believe it's my birthday,' Liv sighs.

'Because?'

'I always thought Matt would be here.' She puts her elbow on the window sill, and puts her chin in her hand.

'Come on, there's millions of cards.' I make her get

dressed and open her cards, and put on her new top and trousers from the parents' joint account which Confers All Gifts, but the trousers are too small or something, so she folds them away to change them. 'Thought you tried them on?'

'Two months ago,' Liv says.

She checks out her new mobile phone, also from the Primary Care Givers. She opens the cards and sighs. 'Sixteen already, I'm old.'

'What's that?'

'A letter.'

'Who from?'

She turns away and reads it through. Her face goes red, then white.

'What is it then?'

'A letter – from Matt – I think he's coming –'

'Let me see.'

'No.'

'What does it say?'

Liv takes a breath and reads: '"*I'm sorry if you misunderstood me the other day. I hope you can forget the things I said so that we can start again.*" He's used the computer, and spell-checked.'

'I'm impressed.' Not.

She goes on trying to read calmly, but the letter shakes and I can tell that the damage is done, by the way she flushes as she reads it: '*What's happened is a good metaphor for a car that looks like a dog, but runs like a dream when you buy it, or the car's a good metaphor for us –*'

'What's he trying to say?'

'*What I'm trying to say is, I'm not as thick as I look. It may be an oxymoron, but unreal real life is the last thing you need for a story, but I understand about background, and so much has happened, lately —*'

'He ate the dictionary — oxymoron?'

'It's only a term pointing up contrasts, like "unreal-stroke-real" life,' Liv says. 'He's really made an effort.'

'What about "background"?'

'He means for my writing. "*Got so much to tell you, it's stranger than truth. Give me another chance, I won't let you down,*" — and he signs it strangely, just "*Car . . . Man*" — or there might be a printer mistake —'

'Matt?' It doesn't seem obvious.

'Of course it's Matt,' Liv says. 'Who else sells cars at the garage?'

'He wrote to you before.'

'Not like this.'

'And you want to go back to the dull years?'

'Matt's not bad.'

'He's not good.'

'I need to believe in this now, all right?' Liv wells up with tears, like she does every day these days. 'What do I have in my life, except school and exams?'

'Family. Friends.'

'And?'

'Me?' I thought I had my sister back, but no. Turn my ignition. See me run back to you. How can you not mind being dumped, then jump-started, like a used car?

I thought she was over the insecure stage. I thought Liv the writer had put away the Liv joined-at-the-hip to Mr

Three-Burgers-At-Once. I thought we could talk about it.

But she won't hear another word, the rest of the day.

At eight, she puts on the shirt-dress and takes it off again.

'Not wearing the chain-belt then?' I'm asking Liv, over *Wuthering Heights*.

'I haven't decided yet,' she says. 'What's he doing now?'

'Heathcliff? Wuthering over Cathy too much – what's the matter?'

'I said,' Liv gasps, '*I haven't decided yet* . . . about anything.' She doubles up for a moment, then straightens and goes to her room.

I read on for a couple of sentences. Heathcliff keeps savage dogs and hangs around swearing at tenants and grieving over Cathy's grave and wanting to join her in it. And all because he, Heathcliff, was abandoned as a baby, so it's not his fault he's bent out of shape and *Wuthering Heights* is pants . . .

Knock, knock. 'Liv – you all right?' I'm trying her door.

She opens, all bright and breezy. 'Of course I am,' she says.

'What haven't you decided about?'

'This one, or this one?' she says, holding up two gross dresses.

'Nothing you want to tell me?'

She looks at me. Says, 'No.'

Later, I bring her a cocktail. 'Drink before you go?'

'Not for me, thanks, no.'

'Not wearing that thing, are you?' I can't believe she's

147

plumped for that baggy old dress, when she was going to look so sophisticated.

'It's fine,' she says. It isn't. 'I'm wearing your earrings – see?'

'But it doesn't even fit.'

'Excuse me for changing my mind,' she says, but she knows it's a lot more than that. The deal was, look good, go out, show Matt Kramer you've got a life, wear the chain-belt anyway, have a blast on your birthday, start a new leaf – instead we have the baggy velvet dress and the kind of soft, reflective Liv we've had for the last month or two, and where's the payback in that? And all because of Matt Kramer, or Matt Kramer's have-me-back letter. 'So what, is he meeting you there?'

'I expect,' Liv says, putting on make-up.

'Did you ring him? How will he know where to go?'

'Sara did – he knows.'

The chain-belt lies on the floor like a pile of broken promises.

'If you're not wearing it,' I probably shouldn't have asked her, 'can I wear your belt to Claire's house?'

Liv shrugs. 'Have it.'

'Moody – what's wrong?'

'If I knew that, I wouldn't be moody, would I?' Tears again, already. 'Can't all be waited on because we're ill all the time.'

'Nice, from the birthday girl.'

'Sorry, I'm in a bad mood.'

Obviously. 'You'll feel better when you get there.'

148

'If I ever get there,' Liv says, changing her make-up again.

Can I have my sister back, please? This is what she's like, when she's under the Matt Kramer 'spell', or should that be smell — motor oil, hair-gel, money, whatever it is. Obviously Matt Kramer has his good points, or Liv would never have gone out with him in the first place. So Matt Kramer looks fit, until the moment he opens his mouth. Still, he must have grown a brain-cell or two. Hitting Liv's interest in writing in an effort to get her back was a dangerous move, as it might just work, unless — 'You know that Matt and Amy Thewliss —'

'I know about Amy Thewliss, so what?' Liv shrugs.

'As long as you do.' Hopefully Thewliss is history. 'Sure you don't want anything?'

'Nothing,' Liv says, lining the inside of her bottom lids with eyeliner, then jumping up and down. 'Ow! Ow! It hurts! Get me a tissue, will you?'

She usually likes a drink before she goes out, but tonight she goes out sober.

'Night, Primary Care Givers,' Liv says.

'Have a good time, Genetic Information Unit,' the parents say, over the sofa, never failing to rise to that one.

'What time was I born?' Liv says.

'About ten minutes to five,' Mum says.

'Did it hurt?'

'Not more than having your head chopped off.'

'So I'm sixteen now,' she says.

We had birthday cake at teatime already, silly cards and

balloons. Liv's sixteen – old enough to want to learn to drive, not old enough for a provisional licence, old enough to drink, not to vote, to get into some clubs, not others. She's almost a Sixth Former now. But as she gets a lift with Sara Bedwell to the meal her mates have planned for her, then on to 'Lime', the hot event, Thursdays at The Mandrake Bar in town . . .

Afterwards I'm going over it, not knowing, but *feeling*, somehow, like Heathcliff, after the Cathy thing went pear-shaped – that there has to be *something* up.

Chapter 17

On the corner next morning, Luke shows off his discman. 'It's a twenty-four track, with introscan –'

'What's introscan?' Beddoes wonders.

'Obvious, innit?' Innit says. 'Intro – in, scan – scans it.'

'– skip-search, and random play,' Luke continues, 'plus I got SXBS.'

'What's SXBS?' asks Beddoes.

'I don't know, do I?' Luke pops the headphones on Bedders' head. 'Get the bass boost yet?' he says, turning it all the way up.

Bedders considers the bass boost. 'Doesn't sound too good.'

He peels off the headset and Innit dons it. 'Stuck, innit?' Innit agrees. 'Playing the same loop, over again.'

'Must be this CD.' Luke tries Back, then Forward. Snapping out the CD, he pops in another. 'This one's all right.'

Innit puts on the headset, stabs Track Select, shakes his head. 'Sticking again – where'd you get it?'

'Odyssey.'

'Bound to stick, then, innit?' Innit hands it back, his jaw

dropping as Paxman breezes out over the junction in a brilliant-yellow puffa, wraparound sunglasses and a Walkman headset. Stabbing a mobile phone, Paxman walks rapidly away up the road without acknowledging them, the brutal haircut combined with the technology about his person making him look strangely bionic – half-man, half-machine.

'Paxman, innit?'

'Get the puffa.' Beddoes' eyes follow it up the road.

'And the shades.'

'Looks like a bee,' Bedders comments.

'Smell a rat?' Luke honks up the road after the puffa. 'Hey, Paxman! What's with doing a carwash when I am?'

Paxman breezes on, in his Walkman. Luke pounds up the road and catches up with him at the Boys' Brigade door, where he pokes him through the puffa. 'WHAT'S WITH MENTAL MIKE?'

Paxman removes his Walkman. 'What?'

'Mental Mike. You're having a laugh.'

'Free market, isn't it?' Paxman says.

'I got in first.'

'Worried, are we?'

'Don't go trying The White Hart. Jim Bowyer's a mate of mine.'

'With a ten-mile radius, I don't need The White Hart,' Paxman says.

'Mummy giving you a lift, is she?'

'That's my business,' Paxman says.

'Stay off my pitches, all right?'

'Ever heard of competition?'

'There's only enough punters for one, and you're not nicking mine.' Luke shoves Paxman against the Boys' Brigade door, where a notice advertising Line Dancing becomes briefly attached to his puffa.

'This is what you do, is it, when you go pushing Danny around?' Paxman says.

'You don't know about Danny,' Luke says. 'Just stay off the carwash –'

'Or what?' Paxman says, straightening to his full height, his face brutal under his crop, his sunglasses showing Luke a small and warped reflection of himself.

'Or you're on to a loser.' Luke shrugs. 'Village is sewn up already.'

'That's what you think,' Paxman says. And coolly walks away.

'I'm the carwash man around here, sad man, loser, freak!' Luke shouts after the disappearing puffa. But as he returns to Beddoes and Innit, Loony Luke wishes he didn't have witnesses to an incident in which he has the uneasy feeling he turned out the loser himself.

Around the bend by White Cottage, Paxman makes a call: 'Danny? He went for it, big time. I think we got him good.'

Luke bobs angrily up to the garage. He crosses the forecourt angrily, in a sweat raised by a stamp up the lane. Opening the shop door, he swings in to hear Matt Kramer's whine: 'I – only borrowed it.'

'A hundred and eighty-five pound, over four weeks?'

The old man's voice is hot with scorn. 'Going to tell me, were you?'

'*Course* I was going to tell you –'

'Don't rob the till again.'

Luke clears his throat, surprising the old man surprising his son over the till with a wad of notes in his hand. 'I'll wait outside, shall I?'

'Give us a minute, Luke, will you?' Old man Kramer looks stricken.

'Course.' Luke shuffles out. Payback time for Kramer makes a little carwashing competition around the village look like a storm in a bucket of suds. He'll probably worm his way out of it. Play on the old man's sympathy. Work extra hard for a while, then slack off. Expect the old man not to notice . . .

Later Kramer crosses his trainers on the desk and opens a magazine. He doesn't feel entirely good, but not entirely bad either. So it didn't look good in front of Couch. So he'll probably have to work hard for a while to get back in the old man's good books, since when did that take longer than a day or two? Still, it gave Couch the edge. About to wind Luke up over the money missing from the till, which he's been happily 'borrowing' himself for some time, Matt now finds the joke's on him.

This doesn't help his self-image.

Even Matthew Abel Kramer gets a queasy feeling in the pit of his stomach when he remembers his father's face as he walked into the garage shop and found him, Matt, over the till. No need to say 'doing a till-balance'. His father had simply walked up to him and stripped the money from his hand. They both knew money had gone missing. Couch *would* walk in on them and see the look on his father's face. I was borrowing it, what a lame excuse. His father had simply looked at him. Don't rob the till again.

Turning another page of his magazine, Matt balances accounts with himself by imagining future successes. So his GCSE grades weren't great last year. Not everyone's a genius like Liv. You could have worked harder, his father had said. You can bet Livvy's got her nose to the grindstone to get good grades next summer. You got to work hard for everything you get in this world. You don't get something for nothing.

But Matthew believes that you do.

Still convinced that he can wing the second year of A Levels without putting in the effort, he scrapes by in maths, dropped French as a stupid idea, hangs on by a thread in geography, looks set to blow out physics, but would breeze through any A Level in imaginary futures.

In Kramer's favourite fantasy, he's a company director with a Lotus Elan behind the office, and can treat the old man to a box at any Grand Prix. At the very least, he's head executive at Moorland Motorbikes & Accessories, with a Kawasaki fifteen-hundred in his very own parking space. For practice, he winds up Luke Couch. Winding up people like Couch enhances his self-esteem . . .

'So Lukey Luke bought something he's pleased with, did he?' Kramer leaves the office and circles Luke outside. 'Give us a look then.'

Reluctantly Luke dries his hands and hands over his compact discman. Kramer weighs the discman in his hand, while Luke watches anxiously over it. 'When d'you get it?'

'Saturday,' Luke says, carefully.

'Gave one like this away to my cousin last week.' Kramer throws the discman from hand to hand. 'Got the Groove Megabass instead. Twenty-four track, rechargeable. Bass boost, plus Skip and Search, SXBS –'

'So how'd it go with your dad?' Luke says.

'– but I don't mind if you want me to keep it.' Kramer puts on the headset, turns up Bass Boost, says, 'DON'T MIND IF I DO', and slopes away over the forecourt, still wearing Luke's discman.

Luke tries not to give Kramer the satisfaction of worrying about it, while he collects valet equipment and slips into the adjoining car showroom to fume silently over a Mitsubishi that Matt's supposed to be grooming. Now that the old man knows that Matt is the leak in the till, he, Luke, could refuse to do Matt's work for him, but the sight of the old man toiling in the chilly, comfortless workshop behind the showroom makes it seem not worth arguing about, and the carwash is slack anyway.

'D'you often get quads in?' Luke asks, entering the chill of the workshop and noticing a mud-splattered quad obviously waiting for repair.

'They usually go down the bike shop,' the old man grunts.

'What happened to this one?'

'Turned over,' the old man says, descending into the inspection pit under a Peugeot.

So the old man doesn't feel like talking. Luke retires to the showroom and puts his back into the Mitsubishi.

After a while, Matt enters the showroom and cruises across to the toilets.

'Let's have it then,' Luke says.

Kramer ignores him. Luke darts to block his way.

'What?' Kramer holds the headset away from his ears.

'I SAID LET'S HAVE MY DISCMAN.'

The top of the old man's head appears above the edge of the inspection pit visible through the door adjoining the workshop, and Matt is lucky enough to spot it.

'Thanks for the loan.' Matt slowly peels off the headset and places it on the vehicle farthest from Luke. 'No need to get out of your pram.'

Later, Luke asks the old man: 'Are quads expensive to fix?'

'Parts is dear. Depends.'

'How about if you put in diesel instead of unleaded? Is it the same as a car?'

'Pretty well,' Mr Kramer says. 'You'll need your engine stripped and cleaned. About Matt and the till, earlier –'

'What about it?' Luke says. 'I forgot all about it.'

Old man Kramer rubs the side of his nose in appreciation of Luke's loss of memory. 'Talk about the wrong fuel, I almost had a court-case once over a mucky pump.'

'What happened?' says Luke, glad the old man feels like talking.

'Matey fills up his four-by-four, when there's muck in the storage tank. Muck goes into the pump, into matey's petrol tank, it messes up his engine, he has to have it towed. Had to settle out of court. Cost me a packet, I tell you. Got to flush out your storage tanks. Hell to pay, if you don't.'

'So diesel in something that takes unleaded –'

'Recoverable, but expensive.'

'What about sugar?' A whisper of something he heard once re-enters Luke's mind. 'Doesn't sugar do something?'

'You don't want sugar in your tank,' says old man Kramer. 'Chemical reaction. Solidifies into a sticky mass. Blocks fuel delivery systems. It don't come up very often, unless someone done it deliberately. Don't know if you noticed, but we don't keep much sugar on the forecourt.'

Used to the old man's dry humour by now, knowing it's a mark of favour, Luke returns to the wash and wax of an engine-parts-salesman's van, picturing as he polishes it something as ordinary as a bag of sugar terminating someone's motor. R.I.P., anything with three lumps, or less. Sugar in your tank, sir? No, ta, I'll just take unleaded. Funny to think that a loaded weapon in the shape of a bag of granulated sits beside the mugs and spoons on the tray in the back of the office . . .

'You never had Mental Mike come round?' Luke chances to Kramer, at the end of the day.

'What are you talking about?' Kramer runs gel through his hair in the office mirror.

'Mental Mike's Mobile Carwash. He just moved in on my business.'

'What d'you expect me to do about it?'

'Keep him off the forecourt?'

'Depends,' says Kramer. 'How much does he pay?'

'Nice,' says Luke. 'I could of told the old man you were robbing the till, but I never.'

'Borrowing on my wages, you mean.' Kramer pauses, gel in mid-air. 'So why didn't you?'

'R-reg black Escort anyone? I'm blocked in,' a customer says, 'if you wouldn't mind moving it?'

Kramer throws his keys at Luke. 'Move the Escort, Couch. And don't leave it over a puddle.'

Luke walks home hot with rage. *Move the Escort, Couch. And don't leave it over a puddle.* Slave to a low-life like Kramer. If he, Luke, wasn't making a packet at Spring Point to buy stuff from Odyssey that was broken, he'd tell him, musclehead, where to get off.

Like anything can dent Kramer's luck. Mister Moneybags has it made. Spring Point has two sister garages in the area, both run by relatives, one of them the Biggest Car Mart In The West. Scum-boy will always have the good things in life. Just what *are* the good things, these days?

Luke turns down the lane he'd swung down with his buckets, the day he'd met Liv, and the tall hedges on either side of the lane had seemed to make a private world in which, for a short time, they could tell one another anything, and no one would judge them. She'd told him – how long ago, now? – she'd wanted Matt, what a joke. And Luke, himself – what had he wanted?

He'd thought he wanted the Odyssey catalogue with bells on, but when he got it, it didn't feel great. Can't always get what you want, Liv had said. For your sake, I hope you don't. Luke pictures telling Kramer to stuff it. The joy of getting the meathead off his back would be balanced against the old man. The old man would rub his nose and say, didn't think you was a quitter.

Can't always have what you want.

Is it worth the pain? Maybe he can afford to drop the garage. Stick with the pub and the village. The carwash went well at The White Hart, where punters were in no hurry while they downed a pint, and inclined to tip generously on leaving. The garage is gold, but so what? Money isn't everything . . .

Luke reaches the end of the long lane stretching down the hill like a muddy ribbon.

Passing the Garden Centre and Mine Row, with Hurst's Nova and a range of A-reg rubbish outside it, he starts down Tree Lane, fiddling crossly with his discman, once again refusing to play anything but a small loop from the same track, over and over again.

The Gamestation hasn't worked since he bought it. The telly's on the blink. The video recorder makes a noise like coughing kittens. Now the discman packs it in. Luke's heart hits rock-bottom as the unwinding hill shows him the valley, and the river snaking away to town, with, somewhere in the distant grey fuzz of the city, another afternoon in Exchange And Refund. Overwork and crap product, Kramer on top of it all – hasn't he suffered enough? *Can't always have what you want.* Good job, if it's from Odyssey. Funny how even – especially – the things that you think are going to be good, turn out to be crap in the end.

Crossly entering the living room when he gets in, looking for someone to blame for his day, Luke finds his father on a chair. 'What's with the chandelier?'

'Broken, I think – can you hold this chair?'

Luke holds the chair and watches his father tinkle in the guts of the plastic chandelier, searching for shattered bulbs. Like he, Luke, doesn't remember Danny stabbing it with a brush, messing around on the table, trying to rub off a scratch.

'Looks as though some of the bulbs are smashed,' Mr Couch says. 'Though how, up here, it could have –'

'He did that ages ago,' Luke says, 'messing around on the table.'

'Who?'

'Danny.'

'Did what?'

'Hit the chandelier.'

'Why was he on the table?'

'Fixing the scratch.'

'What scratch?'

Luke lifts a mat off the table to reveal a livid scratch. 'He did that skateboarding indoors. He puts brown shoe-polish on it, gets on the table with the brush, bashes the chandelier.'

'Wonderful,' says Mr Couch. 'I didn't know someone had broken it. I thought the door had blown shut.'

'He never saw where the end of the brush went.'

'He never sees the end of anything,' says Mr Couch. 'How did you say he made the scratch? No − I don't want to know.'

'He did it doing this experiment, a skateboard on either foot, but he still had these scissors in his hand? − *and* it was Danny who cracked the bog, *and he broke the quad.*'

In the dense moment's silence that follows, the smallest plastic tinkle of the smallest part of the Odyssey chandelier above can quite distinctly be heard.

'He broke the quad?' Mr Couch climbs down from his chair. 'What's wrong with the quad?'

'It won't start, hadn't you noticed?'

Mr Couch examines a very small light bulb. 'What exactly did Danny do to it?'

'Filled it up with diesel, instead of unleaded. Now he's knackered the engine trying to start it.'

'When did this happen?'

'End of term.'

Mr Couch lays down the tiny bulb. 'And you had nothing to do with this?'

'I never broke the light in the barn. Green can's unleaded, you'd have to be blind not to see it −'

'Don't be clever.'

'I'm not.'

'I wondered why you weren't riding it, but Danny told me you were.' Mr Couch looks at Luke. 'Is that all?'

That isn't enough? Luke shrugs. It's dangerous, he can see, to add more. A touch of sarcasm at this point could draw down lightning from the gathering storm in his father's face, which might otherwise still be diverted – on to poor old Danny, unaware, as yet, that the storm is about to break.

'Danny! Got a moment?' Mr Couch yells up the stairs.

'What?'

'Would you come down here, please?'

'I'm doing something, what for?'

The storm-clouds break over the newel-post in the hall, Danny's reluctance to appear beside it making the cloud-burst worse.

'I'm not about to explain myself by *shouting up the stairs*.' Mr Couch goes purple as a very tiny light bulb plummets from the chandelier and smashes, with a tinkling sound, on to the living-room floor. 'If it's not too much trouble for you to come down here, if you don't mind, I'D LIKE A WORD.'

'I can pay for everything,' the voice whispers out of the darkness. 'I can save up my pocket money, plus I can work for the rest.' Danny sobs silently into a fresh pillow, not now stuffed with Luke's smelly socks.

'Sorry I dropped you in it,' Luke whispers back, from the bunk below. 'I was hacked off when I got in. It's Kramer, he's giving me hell.'

'The chandelier would've been fine,' Danny sobs. 'Dad didn't even know it was broken.'

'I know, and I'm *sorry*,' Luke whispers. 'It just came out with the rest.'

'And,' Danny sobs, 'you went . . . and told him about . . . the quad, when I was going to . . . tell him tonight.'

'So you told him now,' Luke says. 'You told him you couldn't see the petrol cans, and he told you, you need glasses.'

'I would of . . . told him . . . myself . . .'

'You probably *do* need glasses –'

'Shut up,' Danny sobs.

Except for the baying of Tiggy Bigglelowe under the moon, the village is silent beyond the window. Hodge the cat watches impassively as Tiggy barks at the moonlight pooling on the Bigglelowes' lawn. *Owf! Owf! Owf!*

'Danno,' Luke says.

'What?'

'I'll help you pay for the quad. I've got loads of money towards it – and I can get the rest.'

'Don't want your money,' Danny sobs. 'I'm getting a job with Mike.'

'You and Paxman – where?'

'None of your business,' Danny says. 'Shut the window, will you?'

Owf-Owf! Owf! Luke shuts the window against Tiggy Bigglelowe and hovers by Danny uncertainly. 'Old man Kramer can fix the quad. Might not be as bad as all that.'

'Go away and shut the door.' Danny turns to the wall and begins to peel tiny strips of wallpaper from a secret edge he's been nurturing beside his bunk.

'Nothing's as bad as sugar, old man Kramer says. And Danny –'

'*What?*'

'I'll tell Dad you were going to tell him.'

'That'll make a difference,' Danny says, in a dead voice.

'I'll say I cracked the bog – *and* I'll pay for the table.'

'I'm tired,' Danny says. 'I want to go to sleep now.' The memory of the pot-plant he knocked down the toilet raises a fresh gust of tears in the dark.

'It'll be all right, I swear it will.'

'*Lukey, please go away.*' The childish whisper through the darkness strips away the years, to a time when they shared a room, and this had been Luke's bunk-bed too.

'No problemo. Night, then.'

No answer but thickening darkness. Quietly closing the door, Luke returns to his room. Methodically repacking the goods from the Odyssey catalogue in their boxes and taping on their receipts, he stacks them in the turquoise carrier bag for a trip to Exchange And Refund.

Not Danny's fault things go wrong. Dad knows things happen to Danny, the reason he went over the Consequences of Hasty Actions gently but firmly. The table would have to be taken to Radstock Wood Crafts to be sanded off and revarnished. The quad would go to a garage. Luke said Spring Point did quads. The chandelier was all right now. But all these repairs cost money.

Danny had sobbed even harder.

So he, Luke, had blown Danny's chance to 'fess up, in a way that he would have hated, himself, if someone had done it to him – he'd given Danny plenty of time to tell Dad himself, hadn't he? Or had he just exploited the situation, and encouraged Danny to drag it out, when he, Luke, knew perfectly well that nothing would fix the quad except telling Dad about it and getting it mended? The circular saw hadn't been his fault. Danny could have confessed at any time.

Still, he shouldn't have jumped in and told Dad like that . . . So he'd been in a foul mood when he got in. So Danny's disasters had been there to take it out on. No excuse made it right again, the way it had been, between them.

He'd give an arm and a leg, right now, to turn back the clock to this morning, when Danny's disasters slept between him and Dad, and no one knew what was broken. Dad didn't like what he'd done. He didn't like it himself.

Luke climbs into bed and stares at the patterns in the wallpaper, remembering the time Danny used to strip bits of wallpaper off the wall when he was about eighteen months old, and he, Luke, had been three. He was probably doing it now, on the other side of the wall . . . he used to stand up in his cot and strip off long strands with his fat hands, until his cot had been moved into the centre of the room and he'd scream for hours in rage . . .

Loony Luke sleeps at last, the other side of the wall from Danny's tear-stained face, and a widening hole in the wallpaper.

Owf! Owf! Owf! The sound of Tiggy Bigglelowe over the road gets mixed up in dreams with Paxman's puffa. A dog wearing that hideous yellow jacket, he thinks that's cool? 'Mental Mike's Dogwash' – that's competition?

Loony Luke talks in his sleep: 'GIVE IT – I shouldna put it – I DON'T KNOW –'

As the village settles down for the night, switches off its tellies at the plug, shuts all the doors against fire, and goes up to bed yawning, the sound of Tiggy Bigglelowe barking away the hours reaches all the way up to the Top Road, where the lights of Spring Point Garage blaze down on an R-reg black Escort parked in a puddle.

Chapter 18

Confessions, Six. We had an upset last night, after Liv got in from her birthday night out, but I'm not going into it here. I crept down at two o'clock and sat on the stairs. Actually it was twenty past two.

I only heard about half of it:

'He turns up –' Liv's voice – 'then chats to *Sara* all night –'

'What did you expect?' Mum says.

'– after he *wrote* to me saying that we should start again –'

'The loose dresses – not *telling* me –'

'I thought we'd get back together.'

'Oh, Liv,' Mum says. 'And you've been to the doctor.'

'Of course.'

'And you think –'

'– *know* –'

'– he doesn't care. Oh, Liv.'

'I can handle it.'

'Liv –'

'Mum. Sit down.'

'Whatever the ins and outs of it, we're not going to

change the facts.' The sound of Dad, putting the kettle on.
'He was at your birthday, and you spoke to him?'

'Briefly.'

'When will you tell him?'

'As if it's not *enough*, he sends me a letter and ignores
me –'

'And you expect us to believe –'

'It isn't anyone's *fault*.'

'You could have told us,' Mum says.

'When I knew, myself.'

'And when you did? Liv, *why*?'

'I needed to think. I don't know.'

You could have told us. Oh, Liv, why? An accident. I
don't know. And round and round, back to the beginning
again. And round and round again. Told you I only heard
half of it. 'Spect you can guess the rest. Happens all the
time. Happened to two girls in my year, a couple of years
younger than Liv. But Liv, of all people, collected and clever
– how could it happen to *her*?

She insists they say nothing to Matt. She'll do it when
she's ready. Yes, she saw Liam Turpitz for a while – no, of
course not – *no* –

'Is there anything else we should know?'

'This isn't enough for now?'

'This is enough for always,' Dad says. 'You've got a lot of
decisions to make.'

Serious matter . . . under-age . . . not when she has it, she
won't be . . . the muttering goes on, deep into the night,
voices rising and falling like the baying of Tiggy Bigglelowe

under some tragic blanket of gloom in my dreams from which he can never surface . . .

Next morning I'm up in the tree before the sun's over the Chapel. If I flip the war-bonnet forwards, I can sit in a nest of feathers with the sunlight sliding between them and warming my legs, a secret world of white, where last night never happened.

A warm, white nest, with sunlight sliding through it, making my legs golden, highlighting stubble and goose-pimples. I would go in and shave my legs, put on my drawstring shorts, but Liv's in the bathroom already. She's in there every morning, dry-heaving over the basin, as the smell of Dad's breakfast wafts up.

Things will never be the same.

But as I said before, I'm not going into it here.

Chapter 19

Nutty Nathan's Carwash
Cheap Rates, Pro. Finish,
Call Nutty Nathan, 768533

So I'm off up the road to The White Hart, Sunday lunch-time, for another day's hard graft, when I see this sign on the Boys' Brigade door, and I feel like I'm going mad. I'm Loony Luke, right? Then Mental Mike. Now *Nutty Nathan*, are you kidding me, or what?

I'm thinking it has to be Beddoes, but why? Probably his idea of a laugh, so I rip down his stupid sign and stuff it through his postbox on my way past his house. Funny, ha, ha, hit me where it hurts, why don't you? I'm thinking of putting the 'Loony Luke' thing to bed next year, if I even do carwash again, when coming up by Mine Row there's only another carwash sign, this time outside Turpitzs' house:

Crazy Chris's Carwash
Contact me, Crazy Chris,
Middlehill 778854

I'll contact him, all right. This is a mate we're talking

about, nicking a prime business idea right from under my feet. What does he think, I won't notice? Thanks a lot, Chris, Innit, idea-thief, whatever you call yourself, these days.

'You can't just nick someone's idea for a business name.' I'm going over what I'm going to tell him, all the way up the path. I'm about to stick it to him, hammering on his front door, ready to pop Innit one, when his mum opens the door instead and says, '*What?*'

'Is Innit in?' I'm asking her.

'If you mean Chris, he's out.'

I bet he is. 'You sure?'

Mrs Turpitz, ugliest woman in the universe, tries to turn her neck, which looks like pork tied with string. Even Mum says that Mrs Turpitz has every disadvantage known to man, meaning weight, chins, moles, elephant legs, attitude and Innit for a son, though big brother Liam and Liv, some people say they went out –

'CHRIS!' she bawls up the stairs. She turns back and gives me her wall eye. 'I think,' she goes, 'I'd know.'

'How long's he been doing the carwash?'

'Don't want no carwash.'

'I know *you* don't. Crazy Chris, is he doing one, I mean?'

'Don't come here teasing about carwash,' Mrs Turpitz says, going red.

'There's a sign outside that says Chris washes cars.'

'Only car Chris ever washed is the one he backed into the hedge when his uncle stayed last year,' goes Mrs Turpitz moodily, with the sun shining off her moustache. 'Anything else, or that do you?'

'Can he call me – it's business.'

'Don't you tell *me* to mind my own business.'

'Sorry?'

'What are you saying?' She glares. Did I say she's a bit deaf, as well?

'Can – Chris – call – *me*, Loony –'

'Loony, now, is it?' she goes. 'Get off, or I'll loony you –'

'You don't understand, I –'

'Get out of it!' Mrs Turpitz clumps down the steps and throws out her big purple arm. 'Go on, get off, you cheeky beggar!'

I'm out of the gate and gone, but Mrs Turpitz tanks after me down the path. She rips down the 'Crazy Chris' sign off the gate and throws it in the road. 'Don't you come round here with your tricks!' She's too big to run far, which is good, being as the thing I'm running fastest from is the idea she'll trip and roll over me.

'*And don't you come back!*' she shouts, huffing in the middle of the road like a beetroot. I think she must've gone mad.

I'm still not sure what happened when I get up the road by the Garden Centre. I wouldn't mind, but I never *did* anything to make her chase me, or rip down the sign saying '*Crazy Chris's Carwash*' that Innit put up, not me. She should watch out for a heart-attack. Going red and chasing people when they just want to know who pinched their idea. Lucky for him he was out, or 'Crazy Chris' might have copped it.

I'm wondering if *I'll* cop some good tips today – The White Hart does well over lunchtimes – when Mental Mike shows up on the other side of the Garden Centre wall, hosing plants in boxes.

'Yo, Paxman, stolen anyone else's business ideas lately?'

'Want to make something of it?' he goes, waving the hose around. 'Who's on the wrong end of the hose this time? Looks like the tables are turned.'

'Tables turned, Simpkins, pip, pip!' I'm doing the old World-War-Two aeroplane with my arms. 'Spod at three o'clock – prepare to fire!'

Paxman sprays the hose in the road, dumping a huge wet stripe on the tarmac.

'Near miss! Return fire, Simpkins!' I give him a clod of earth over the wall.

'Funny man,' he says. And he gives me the hose full-on.

'Waterproofs, Paxman, you loser!' The water thuds into my back. Lucky for him I'm dressed for the carwash, or I'd have to stuff his head in a bucket. Danny's killing himself in the greenhouse behind Paxman. Thanks a lot, laughing boy, when I'm working to pay off your debts. 'Enjoy yourself, why don't you – hey, Danny – what are you doing here?'

'Working, what do you think?' Paxman says, loading plants into a wheelbarrow.

'You got him a job?'

'Away from you.'

Dan pops out of the greenhouse. 'Just a bit wet, then.'

'Thanks to your big mate here, Paxman.'

'Wash off the smell,' Danny says. Nice, in front of Paxman.

'Working with sad-boy, are we?'

'Pays me,' says Danny. 'Why not?'

'Because you like gardening so much.'

'Leave me alone,' says Danny.

'Moonlighting or something, Paxman?'

'What?'

'Carwashing *and* the Garden Centre – what about Mental Mike's Carwash?'

'Slow, isn't he?' Paxman goes to Danny.

Danny makes a face. 'Mental Mike. Nutty Nathan. Contact Crazy Chris.'

'You mean – it was a *wind-up*?'

'Mrs Turpitz chase you down the road, did she?' Paxman's killing himself. 'Hope you ran fast enough.'

'But why –'

'Innit got Ben Dent and Dominic to cold-call about car-washes already. Guess she was ready to blow,' Danny yuks, and she *was* a bit like a volcano.

'What, they put up the signs?'

'The signs were my idea,' Danny goes.

'Thanks for nothing, bro'.'

'You shouldn't have dobbed me in,' Danny goes. 'You can stuff your money, I don't need your help. And you shouldn't have laughed at my chicken.'

'What, Henny-Penny?'

'She couldn't fly. She tried to escape up a tree, and *you* thought it was funny when the fox took her in the night and went and et her.'

'She was half-dead and she couldn't lay eggs – what d'you *want* me to do?'

175

'Not laugh? I *hate* you sometimes.'

Paxman's loving it. 'Go Danny, go Danny –'

'Shut it, Paxman,' I'm telling him. 'Anyone ever tell you, you look like a prat in that puffa?'

As I'm walking away my wet waterproofs give me a giant wedgie, but I'm not about to sort it until I get round the corner. Can you *believe* Danny? When I'm only slaving to pay off the quad, the chandelier and the table for him, and he doesn't even care. And I don't want to *go* up the pub and wash cars any more, and I'm tired from Mrs Turpitz and the weight of my stupid wet clothes, and most of all, from Danny.

'I'll see *you* later,' I'm shouting back. But he doesn't even hear me. So Paxman works at the Garden Centre, where Mummy fixed it for him . . .

At least I'm still the only carwash in town, now I know 'Nutty Nathan' and 'Crazy Chris' are only stupid signs, while Paxman has to work for Dave Venning, wheeling plants around and talking to oldies about south-facing walls and gulches, or is it mulches?

Learning the posh names of plants, that'd be right up his street. Mental Mike – like Paxman could run his own business. There's more to being self-employed than you think. You have to be your own boss. Work out your own schedule. Collect the money, keep accounts, plus there's no security and work could dry up, any day.

Good job if Paxman *does* work at the Garden Centre, getting three-twenty an hour in the Land That Time Forgot, boring people to death and growing mould over his boots, he stood in one place so long, yakking. Danny can grow mould too. He never told me he had a job. He never even talks to me now.

So Paxman gets a holiday job learning to be sadder than he already is. He isn't out on the carwash, and that's what makes my day.

From twelve to two at The White Hart, I wash seven cars and a motorbike. On the way home from the pub I'm so knackered I can hardly see. I don't even notice it, at first. But the new sign on the Boys' Brigade door is a bit of a puzzler this time:

Missing
German Shepherd cross
Answers to
'Tiggy'
Last seen Middlehill Monday night
Ring Bigglelowe on 776854

Thought it had gone a bit quiet.

Chapter 20

Fifth week of the holidays, and the last week in August. Up at Kitty's Kitchen, the dismal little café on the Top Road, a girl in a floppy hat scribbles busily in an exercise book. She's there almost every lunchtime, writing as though she means it.

Today her Lunchtime Special congeals beside her arm as her hand rapidly covers the page. Her hair and her hat hide her face. A long summer dress hides her figure. She writes and revises in earnest now, from one until two o'clock, daily. Slowly at first, and then faster, the ideas are teased out and changed.

The sun beats down on the Top Road, and the Tangle Twisters melt very slightly in the labouring freezer at the newsagent's, where the owner, Di, eats a very bad pasty and covers for Liv during the lunch-hour.

Matt Kramer idles at Spring Point Garage, a quarter of a mile up the road. The sun cooks the wine gums in their greasy bags by the till. Matt has a headache this morning from a night out at Dance Academy. The long, idle stretch of lunchtime, and the holidays generally, seem to have done in his brain. He can't be bothered to look through *What Car*, the reflected heat from the window having knocked his thoughts into neutral. Not even teasing Luke Couch can put his brain into gear. It's no fun when his father defends him.

'Least the boy sticks to something,' is his father's only idea about Couch, as though *sticking to things* is a career.

Sticking to things is something Matt Kramer can't do.

He stuck with the idea of accountancy in the Lower Sixth, until maths grades became a problem. He thought about a professional car-cleaning service only quite recently – New Pin Valet & Car Care – after Luke came up with the carwash, but stuck with it only two days when the old man pointed out how much organization would be involved.

His father suggested a business studies course, but Kramer stuck with that for less time than it took to suggest it. He stuck with golf for as long as it took to buy a full set of clubs, then sold them for more than he paid for them. What's the point in Business Studies when the garage will come to him anyway, and he can stick a stooge like Couch in the office and get down to power boat racing? The old man has to retire one day, sooner the better for the show-room, which needs some *seriously* classy motors to step it up league. Reviewing *What Car*'s Top Twenty Convertibles, Matt makes his imaginary selection. Definitely the Cobra. Probably the Lotus Elise, though the streamlining's a little showy.

Looking up through the sun glare, he sees Liv Bickle sail by in a dress, and all sorts of odd feelings surface. Looking

179

daggy, but still the way she walks reaches out and touches him. *Liv, wait!* Something in him swims out to meet her. Then she's passed by, and it's gone. Still his thoughts follow her, out on to the dusty pavement, where the traffic beats by, and the newsagent waits to receive her.

Liv — it's me!

With a sense of relief Matt loses her as a customer enters the shop. 'Fifteen-thirty on pump five? Would you like a receipt for that?'

The transaction over a debit card blots out the glowing figure in a flowing dress. *Liv. It's me.* So what. So they were good together. Sticking with someone for a lifetime. Who would want to do that?

Chapter 21

Exchange And Refund goes OK. Odyssey isn't even that busy, so I only have to wait for a man to change a shaver and a woman to take back a bottle-warming thing before I can try for a refund.

'Name?' the girl says.

'Luke Couch.'

'And what would be wrong with the products?'

'Parents got them already.' I'm lumping the bag on the counter.

'What – everything?'

'Yeah.'

'What was it, your birthday?'

'That's right.'

She looks at me for a minute. Then she fills in the refund form.

'Did you pay by credit card?'

'Cash.'

'So you want a full refund?'

'Please.'

'And you don't want to keep anything?'

'No.'

I can't be bothered to explain that it's all cack – bashed telly with no aerial, scratched watch, whizzy video recorder, useless Gamestation console that won't load games. The assistant stacks the boxes behind the counter and hands me the cash from the till. When I turn round, the boxes are gone. They probably went back up the chute so somebody else can buy them, then take them back again. Probably someone else had that stuff before I did. Once you're in the circle of cackness, there's no way out but being skint. So I shouldn't have been noticing Toys & Pushchairs, next to Portable Compact Disc Players, in the catalogue, on the way out.

Once I noticed, I had to look. Once I looked, I found this cute baby toy and filled in an order form. Once I filled in an order form, I had to go and pay at the till. Once I'd paid at the till, I had to join the queue in Chairs. So Odyssey got me again, round and round and round.

'Order number *five hundred and eighty*, to your Collection Point, please.'

That's me. Collection Point A's pretty swift.

'Number eight-oh-eight-three-five.' The girl looks at me. 'Baby Mobile with Colourful Toys and Mirrors to Visually Stimulate Your Child?'

'Yeah, it's cute.'

'Present, is it?'

'No, I want to play with it myself.'

'So will you want giftwrap with that?'

'No, ta.' No way am I waiting while she wraps it in slow-mo, plus I *do* want to play with it myself.

'And would you be interested in a ten-per-cent discount on a matching themed cot-buffer and mattress?'

Do I look like I would? 'I dunno, what is a cot-buffer?'

'It protects baby's head in his cot.'

'Just the mobile, thanks. And the Groove Megabass.'

Chancing a new discman here, the model Kramer's got. I reckon I deserve something for bringing the rest back to Odyssey.

The assistant checks my receipt. 'Sign here.'

I check out the Baby Mobile as soon as I leave the shop. A couple of people are staring at me – *what*? Never seen anyone fourteen buy a gift for a baby before?

Still, you wouldn't want to meet Hurst or Beddoes, carrying a Baby Mobile to Visually Stimulate Your Child. The mobile's pretty embarrassing, even in its Odyssey bag. Good that it's under wraps and not too big.

Good job I told Dan I'd meet him at two. He went off with Mum somewhere.

'Fuzzy world's gone,' Danny goes, when I meet him outside the Vision Centre in a slimline pair of glasses. 'I can see everything really sharply. I didn't know trees had edges.'

'Are you having a laugh?' He isn't. 'I didn't know you were going to get glasses.'

'Neither did we,' Mum says. 'Vision Centre gave him an

eye test. They said he should've had glasses ages ago. It's my fault. I feel really guilty.'

They actually don't look that bad. 'You shouldn't've done that,' I'm going. 'Now he thinks he looks clever.'

'I can see your face, Luke,' he's going. 'And I can see the leaves. I didn't know you could see leaves, I thought trees were just blobby things.'

Mum's looking at me. I'm looking at her. 'I can't believe I didn't realize.'

'You realized now,' I'm saying.

Old Danny can't get enough of looking at things. He looks at the pistachio nuts in the health food shop. He looks at the Pick 'n' Mix in Woolworth's. He looks at trainers in the sports shop like he never saw 'em before. He looks down the street. 'Look at that!'

'What?'

'The cars,' he says, 'they've got doors!'

I never thought that he might not be able to see. I mean, really not see. 'So d'you have to wear glasses all the time?'

'Only if I want to see.'

'Don't wear 'em on the school bus.'

'I can see everyone's faces,' he goes. 'Before they were just pink blobs. Now they've got eyes and a nose.'

'At least you're in Sharp World now,' Mum goes. 'And those metal frames look nice.'

All the way home, he's looking at stuff from the car. When we get home, I give Dan some of the refund money.

He looks at it. 'Two hundred quid?'

'Should pay for the table and some of the quad.'

'I told you, I don't want your money,' he goes. 'I can pay off the quad myself.'

'It's only money,' I'm telling him. 'Pay it back when you like.'

Danny looks at the money. 'Dad'll ask me where I got it from.'

'Tell him you got a pay rise. Pay it back in instalments, like you earned it.'

'I *am* earning it.'

'I know you are, this is just quicker.'

Danny looks at me. 'Don't *you* want to spend it?'

'I did, and now I got it back.'

'About the Crazy Chris thing —' Danny picks up the money — 'all that stuff with Paxman —'

'Geekus Maximus doesn't bother me.'

'It was just a joke,' Danny goes.

'Forget it.'

'Yeah?'

'What do you think?'

Danny puts on the telly and watches it through his glasses, and for the first time in weeks, accounts balance up between us. Debit, me telling Dad he broke stuff. Credit, me paying for it, for him — except that there's more to it than that. A dead chicken, and feeling sorry that I wound him up over it, is in there somewhere.

'So do I tell Dad you lent it to me?' Danny goes, after a while.

'Only if you want,' I'm saying. 'He'll let you off soon anyway.'

Danny switches channels. 'You reckon?'

'Wait till he hears you need glasses, you won't see repayments again.'

Danny fans out his wad. 'Want to bet on that?'

'He sees the glasses, it's in the bag. Tenner says Dad caves.'

'Edward Elgar's head says he won't,' says Danny, fascinated with the look of the twenties I lent him, now he can see the detail.

The accounts balance up between us, no matter which way you look, and if they don't, who cares about money? Seeing Danny watch telly in focus for the first time ever has to make me realize how long he spent in Fuzzy World, and I'd blow everything I got from the carwash if it meant Danny could go back in time and see everything he missed.

'What's the house look like then?' I'm asking him every five minutes.

'Things look funny,' he goes. 'Like, grainy, with bits everywhere. Plus I can see where the forks are.'

'You won't muddle up the petrol cans now,' I'm reminding him. 'Mistake the red can for the green can, I mean.'

His face drops when I mention the quad, so I whip off his glasses and try 'em. 'Look intellectual, do I?'

'Like Luke in glasses,' Danny says, putting them on again carefully.

'I blame myself,' Dad goes, when he gets in. 'Should've realized the boy needed glasses when he moaned about the blackboard at school.'

'Optician said he had minus-four vision in the left eye, slightly more in the right,' Mum goes, blaming herself.

I'm winking at Danny. Hey up.

'Can't expect the boy to contribute to damage he caused when he couldn't *see*,' Dad goes.

'Should've taken him for an eye test years ago,' Mum agrees.

'That's why he didn't spot that castor going under the saw.'

'Ben Dent wears glasses,' Mum goes. 'But somehow, I didn't think.'

'The quad, of course –'

'They make some nice glasses now.'

'– no wonder he mixed up the fuel. It's dark under the bench in the barn.'

'Even contact lenses aren't as expensive as you think.'

'I can't see underneath it myself.'

'They wondered how he managed to read –'

'It's a wonder he didn't hurt himself, messing about with that saw. It's us,' Dad goes, 'at fault, here. Funny we couldn't *see* it.'

Repayments over, I win. I'm winking at Dan like mad. You owe me, told you so – I'm laughing, you're twenty quid down.

Later I go upstairs and lock the door to my room and try out the Megabass, which is wicked. Then I pull out the baby mobile from under the bed and fit those colourful mirrors on to the wire frame, thread on plastic cows and pigs, and set the whole thing spinning. It's easy to hook it over the curtain rail. Then I can lie back and watch the mirrors go round in the breeze from the window . . .

Clack, clack, the plastic animals go round, the mirrors flashing, little bells on 'em tinkling. And it's quiet – so quiet – with the little, tinkling bells and the plastic dogs and cats and cows and pigs, meeting and parting, meeting and parting, and no Tiggy Bigglelowe barking, and time just to lie there and think . . .

'Luke? You in there?'

'What?'

'Tea,' Dan goes.

'Already? I never heard the gong.'

I'm cool about cottage pie, even though it's the first time we had it since the rotten mince thing in Dan's cupboard, and I think it's those plastic dogs, meeting and parting and meeting again, that's making me feel calm inside. Imagine what they must look like if you're a baby and you don't understand what they are, but the shapes go round and round and they look sort of bright and interesting, and still they go clacking, clacking, changing shape as they go . . .

'You're quiet, Luke,' Dad goes.

'Things to think about.'

'How's business?'

'Good.'

'Funny about Tiggy Bigglelowe,' Mum says. 'Slipping his leash in the night.'

'Funny,' I'm going.

'Quiet, though.'

'Yeah.'

'Lovely and quiet,' Mum goes.

After tea, in the quiet summer evening, Danny and I feed the chickens, and Danny remembers their names, now he can see which one's which:

'Sukey, Hattie, Lucy – see, she's got that white feather? I never knew she had a white feather. Is that one Patchy? And Stick-feet! Look how big Stick-feet is! Beaky and Eggy are huge! Did One-eye always have black round her beak? I never saw that one before, is it Molly? Look at Groggy, Luke – is that one Groggy, Luke?'

'Yeah,' I say. 'Funny legs. Always looked like that.'

Mad to think he couldn't really see 'em before. No wonder he never fed them. They looked like blobs on legs.

The baby mobile's still tinkling in the breeze when I go up to bed. I'll put it away in the morning. Till then it reminds me of Danny and me when we were little. The time he broke my water-gun. The time he fell in the nettles and broke the toilet flush. He broke a lot of things. And the toy dogs walk round in the breeze, the mirrors flash and tinkle, and meet, and part, and meet . . .

Then there was Danny and the wallpaper, on summer evenings like this one that I can only just remember, when I was about three and a half. I can remember seeing Danny standing up in his cot in a blue nightsuit, stripping bits of wallpaper off the wall, and knowing I should get Mum.

'Naughty,' I'd go, when we were in bed, and he'd start.

'Stipping,' he'd go, which meant 'stripping'.

'Not stipping.'

'*Stipping.*' And he'd pull off little strips of wallpaper, leaning over the edge of his cot.

'Mum!' I'd yell. 'Danny's stipping!'

And up the stairs she'd come and move Danny's cot away from the wall, till he ended up in the middle of the room, and would he scream for hours . . .

I think he does 'stipping' now. I've seen the hole in the wallpaper beside his bed. When he's grown up he can buy a whole house and peel off the wallpaper, if he wants.

For ages we still had the wallpaper Danny tore. I can see the pattern now, hundreds of little cars running up and down a trellis — is it a trellis? It makes me feel a bit sad to think about baby things. Quiet times, when I was little. Times, even, before Danny was born, when I was a baby myself, and everything was blurry and pink, and I lived in Fuzzy World.

Babies are cute, I suppose. I imagine her face when I give her the mobile, and I know what money's for. The baby toy's for her, did I say? Nothing to do with Danny and me, or times when we were little. Nothing to do with anyone else.

I heard something about Liv Bickle.

Chapter 22

'Tig – Tig –Tiggy! Tig – Tig – Tiggy!'

Tiggy Bigglelowe disappeared two weeks ago, and no one's seen him since. Instead of constant barking, we now have Mrs Bigglelowe calling him all the time: 'Ti-ggy! Tig-Tig-Tig! You 'aven't seen him, Sylvia, 'ave you?'

'Sorry, Mrs Bigglelowe.'

'Dunno if I'll ever see him again now.' She wrings her hands, but she's such a witch you can't feel sorry for her. 'Tiggy, my darlin', where are you?'

Hopefully twenty miles away. Or maybe under a bus.

The school bus turns up this week, fresh for the start of a new academic year, with more potential safety hazards than usual. I'm talking overcrowding, no seat belts, overheating engine, illegal exhaust, dodgy brakes, interior filth and a psychopathic driver. Apart from that, it's fine. Years Seven to Nine went back already. I go back on Tuesday, Liv's going when she can face it.

Meanwhile, Friday today, and Liv says: 'Lakey Park.'

'Lakey Park?'

'Got anything else planned?'

'Weather's not great.'

'So what?'

September now, and the wind through the tree feels cool, and the leaves look tired and yellow.

'Coming?' Liv appears like a rose at the bottom of the stairs, plump and pink and blooming.

I pull on a jumper. 'Why not?'

So we hop the bus to Lakey Park and everything seems so easy and fun, I say, 'We should do this more often.'

She leans on my arm as we pass her old school, near where we used to live, a house I hardly remember. Funny to think Liv was alive for almost two years before I even existed. And I'm glad I decided to come, to spend time with the Liv I don't know, a part of her that grew up here before I was born.

Entering Park Gates feels weird, even to me.

Everything seems smaller and sadder. The cricket field stretches away to the now cruel-looking Children's Zoo, thankfully closed and empty of neurotic animals, the too-small enclosures filled with rubbish, the sheds spotted with bird-droppings. Beyond the Swan Lake Café a few Canada Geese sit on the duckpond, where Liv famously fell through the ice one winter, ice-skating with Christine, her friend who lived near the park.

'Remember Christine?'

'Do you?' Liv says.

'Only just.' Actually I only remember her as plaits and fingernails. 'Was the Children's Zoo always that small?'

'I think so,' says Liv. 'Funny how it didn't seem cruel then.'

'Maybe it wasn't then, but it would be now.'

'What do you mean?

'The feeling – and the time – are the same.' I can't explain it. 'Now it's a different place.'

'Freezing, isn't it?' Liv says.

A cold wind blows off the lake from the harbour beyond. Beyond the harbour, Evening Hill looks bleak amongst its pines.

'Closed for winter, already – I used to love that train.' I'm pointing out the sign by the miniature station. 'End of Season Service, Saturdays Only.' The miniature train itself would be tucked up in its shed by the bamboo clumps, on the other side of the duckpond.

'Lucky for you,' Liv says, 'or we'd've had to've had a go on it.'

'Warm enough in that jumper?'

'Come on,' Liv says, 'let's walk.'

So we walk round the edge of the lake, and she picks out the swans' feathers bobbing in the end-of-season rubbish. 'Big ones!' She holds one up.

'They stink, don't they?'

'Soon wash them off. Got a bag?'

'Think I might have – yes!'

Soon we're hooked on collecting feathers. Just one more turn, round the next little bay, just one more look in a nook, and the next nook filled with rushes, scum and lolly sticks, and the next, and the one after that . . . In no time we're past the twisted pine and opposite the bowling green. And the day seems bright and special as the wind cuts across from the harbour, and we reach the paddle-boats.

'Remember these?' Liv says. 'We went in them when we were kids.'

I vaguely remember them. 'Just about.'

'Let's take one out.'

'You're not serious?'

'Come on,' she laughs. 'Why not?'

So we stop at the booth and pay, and a woman in an anorak leads us down to the boats, huddled in their pool like sheep against the boom cutting them off from the lake. As we climb into a boat they seem smaller than I seem to remember them, low in the water with our weight, not so much fun any more. 'You sure about this?'

'Grab a handle,' Liv says, churning away with hers and screwing us sideways. With their miniature 'paddle steamer' wheels at each side, the paddle-boats are pretty bizarre. *Veronica*, ours is called – number twenty-four.

'Paddle,' says Liv. 'Come on!'

I'm turning my handle like mad, and my paddle goes round and the grey-green water boils up as slowly we leave the other boats named *Peaches*, *Irene* and *Cherie* and nose out over the boat pond.

'Go in a straight line!' says Liv, splashing me as she changes direction.

'Straight line yourself,' I'm saying, showering her back and pumping my handle round.

'Stop splashing me!' Liv shouts. 'Turn the same way I am!'

'I *am* turning the same way you are –'

'Will you stop?' Liv says, splashing me deliberately.

'I'm not doing anything – thanks!'

What with the paddles, and trying to steer, we're killing ourselves laughing before we reach the inflatable boom dividing the boat pond from the lake.

'The swans think we're mad,' Liv says.

Maybe we are. What a grey day to come out. A couple of swans bobbing between us and Swans Island are the only other things on the lake. The wind's hitting us directly now that we've cleared the Point sheltering the boat pond, and slightly more serious waves are slapping into the side of the boat. Beyond the boom blocking our way out on to the lake, the waves are even bigger.

'Let's go back now, it's cold.'

'Not yet,' Liv says. 'Let's go on.' She churns her handle right up to the inflatable boom, and without stopping she lifts it, ducks under it, and drops it behind the boat in a shower of water.

'Liv, we can't *do* this!'

'Just did.'

'We can't go out on the lake!'

'Why not, we always used to.' Liv turns to look ahead. 'When I was a kid, you could go wherever you wanted. Paddle, or we'll go round in circles.'

Veronica dips like a swallow now that the boom doesn't protect us from lake-sized waves any more. The wind tears through our clothes. Water spurts over the side and whole waves smack into the boat. 'Liv – please – let's go back!'

195

'Paddle,' she says, 'or we'll sink.'

Out on to the steely grey lake we go, churning against the waves, passing the swans bobbing a little way away from us, wondering what we're doing there. With no time to wonder ourselves, it takes an incredible effort to make any headway at all. Churn, churn, churn. Gradually the Swan Lake Café grows smaller over my shoulder, and the boulders of Swans Island, almost in the middle of the lake, grow larger behind Liv's head.

'You turn now,' Liv says. 'I'll stop.'

'Why, where are we going?'

'Turn,' Liv says, again.

Steely little waves smash into us as Liv tries to bring us about.

'Liv, I'm scared, I want to go back!'

'Keep going, we're almost there!' Liv joins me and we both turn together. At last the wind drops away as we come into the lee of Swans Island, and I can see now that she's making for it.

'The current'll take us past it!' I can feel it tugging against us.

'You turn – now me – now both together, go!' Liv's wet hair lashes her face as she turns to and fro to aim for the island.

And somehow we're making way by a miracle, Liv with her tummy, me with my glandular fever, me shouting at her, her shouting back, in the middle of the lake at Lakey Park, on a chilly Friday morning in September.

'You shouldn't be doing this!'

'What — in my condition, you mean?' Liv grins and paddles harder, as at last we curl in on a grim little beach made of imported grey sand. Spray hits us as we come about, the sky seems to frown on *Veronica*, the wind whips cold and bitter. Liv looks round for a place to land. 'More paddling on your side — Sylvie, try harder, come on!'

'You're not going to land?'

'Why not?'

'Paddle-boat man must be going ballistic —' No point in arguing now, as *Veronica* grounds on the sand. 'You're not getting out?'

'Not for long.'

Liv clambers out and I haul up the boat on the 'beach'.

'Not exactly Paradise Island, is it? Liv, are you all right?'

'Just a bit out of breath.' Liv hangs her head and recovers.

The artificial beach slopes up to an ugly island made of boulders netted in cages and streaked with droppings. Bits of swans' eggs, untidy nests left over from the breeding season, feathers everywhere. 'Looks better from a distance, doesn't it?'

'You get . . . the best feathers here,' Liv says.

'You came here before?'

'This was our dream place to get them — me and Christine and Vicky. They made it for swans to nest on.' Liv straightens, at last. 'Wonder where they are now?'

'The swans?'

'Christine and Vicky. Seemed easier to get here then.'

Swans appear from behind boulders, flapping their wings and throwing up their necks to tell us off for waking them up. One of them snaps at another as it goes by.

'Crabby lot, aren't they?'

'They can be quite nasty,' Liv says. 'But there again, it's their island.'

Swans resting above the beach get up and waddle off, wagging their tails in disgust. Others, asleep on one leg, lift their heads from under their wings and re-enter the water. Something takes off from the beach like a gun-shot, exploding over the lake in a flurry of flapping wings. Something makes a honking noise: *Go! Go! Go!*

'What a fuss,' Liv says.

'I thought swans were mute.'

'That was a goose,' Liv says. 'But the swans used to hiss at us.'

'We shouldn't be here disturbing them.'

'It seemed all right, at the time –'

'Paddle-boat man's coming out.' I can see him, shading my eyes. 'He's waving. I think we should go – Liv, where are you going?'

'Won't be a minute,' she says.

I'm lecturing her about getting back into *Veronica* right now, when out of a grim pile of stones, Liv pulls a rusty old jar: 'I knew it would still be here!'

'What is it?'

'Something we buried ages ago, if I can . . . *open* it.'

'Let me.' Anything to get her back in the boat. It takes me all my strength to open the cruddy old jar. Inside there's a plastic bag and, inside the bag, a piece of paper. 'This what you want?'

Liv unrolls it. 'Still dry, that's amazing.'

'Read it in the boat.'

'But I've got to put it back.'

'Liv, we've got to go now.'

But first she shows me the message in the bottle.

'Look,' she says, 'see this?'

We, the Undersigned, Olivia Jane Bickle, Christine Mary Hawdon and Victoria Louise Gates, Hereby Promise to Stay Friends for Ever and Ever, No Matter What.

To Which We Put Our Hand This Sixth Day of August, 1995:

Olivia Jane Bickle
Christine Mary Hawdon
Victoria Louise Gates

'Shouldn't that read, "to which we put our hands", not hand?'

'That bit was my idea.' Liv grins. 'I still sign my name the same.'

'Can't believe you left it here six years ago.'

'We promised to leave it for ever. Meet in the park in ten years' time, same day, sixth of August.'

'So Christine –'

'Don't know where she is.'

'Vicky?'

'Don't want to know. She had an accident in the bath

199

while we were all in it once, having a fit of giggles, farting for laughs, when suddenly –'

'Revolting girl.'

'We were only eight.'

'Clearly the pact is broken. Come on, it's the paddle-boat man!'

But I can't make her come until she's stuffed a new piece of paper inside the jar and screwed it up and buried it under the boulders, in the same place as before.

'What is it?'

'A new message, promise, pact – whatever you want to call it.' Liv dusts off her hands, flushed but satisfied. 'I remember this island,' she says. 'I remember *myself*, as I was. Like me and the island, together – like it and me make a *land*.'

'I know what you mean.' The memory of coming to the park myself when I was four, having an ice cream, riding on the train, coming on these paddle-boats, is so completely weird for a moment that the lake seems to rush away from me in time, like travelling away from myself. 'Time is a place, I suppose – like the park.'

'Nice,' Liv says. 'I might use that.'

'Your time is up, number twenty-four!' A dinghy curls in on the beach.

Liv starts for the boat, but he stops us. Hailing us with a whistle, the paddle-boat man cuts his engine and glides between us and *Veronica*.

'Don't you move a muscle – you two girls – wait there!'

*

The paddle-boat man actually rescues us and gives us a ride to the jetty. If we didn't know we needed rescuing before, we know it after he tells us: 'Dangerous thing to do, coming out on the lake. Can't let you go back in the leisure craft.'

'The paddle-boat, you mean? Why not?' Liv says.

'I can't have you ending up at the bottom of the lake. I got insurance to think about.'

'You mean,' Liv says, 'we might have sunk?'

'Lost the *Phoebe*, last year. Can't risk losing another, or we won't have no twenty-four.'

'Twenty-four what?'

'*Veronica*.' He points to her number. 'Painted her up, last year.'

Veronica bobs behind us, in the wake of the RIB – a Rigid Inflatable Boat, the paddle-boat man tells us. Made for picking up idiots who ought to know better, he says.

'It felt a bit scary,' Liv says, 'but I thought it would be all right because we *used* to take paddle-boats out on the lake –'

'That was before they built the pumping station.' He points it out, an ugly concrete tower on the embankment between the lake and the harbour.

Liv shrugs. 'What does that do?'

'Alters the flow of water. It goes in and out to the sewage farm, and a lot more comes in from the harbour. There's strong currents, some times of day.'

'So what we did – it was dangerous?'

'Dangerous, you could say.'

Other words hang in the air. Not entirely our fault, I want to say. Liv had thought it was all right, safe in her memories of going out on to the lake when no boom closed in the boats. Now it's a different time, a different place, with different rules, and a different me and Liv, not deliberately reckless.

'We thought your boom was fussy,' Liv says. 'Sorry we made you come out.'

'You won't be the last,' the paddle-boat man says, killing the outboard by the booth.

The woman in the anorak's waiting for us. 'What d'you think the boom's for?'

'Sorry?'

'It's idiots like you that get us closed down.'

'We didn't know it wasn't safe –'

'We're not insured for the lake,' she snaps. 'You mind you don't come back.'

Liv and I leave in disgrace.

'Banned from the paddle-boats, oh no, how will we live it down?' she says, as soon as we get round the corner.

'You're so *bad*,' I tell her.

'I remembered it wrong, so what?'

'So you might have sunk us?'

She knows she actually might have. 'It was all right.'

'Even so.'

The Coke in the Swan Lake Café tastes even better for being out of the wind. Stony Swans Island looks impossibly far out over the lake. Hard to believe we could have got there in a paddle-boat, mad even to try it. Through the raindrops hitting the window the lake seems more unwelcoming, the island disappearing through the grey mist of rain. And we know now that it was dangerous to have gone there, but still it seems dramatic to have buried a secret message out there, and to know that it's probably there always, now no one can go there, any more.

'So what did it say?'

Liv's eyes widen over her straw.

'Come on, your new message, what was it?'

Liv looks out on the steely lake. 'Secret,' she says.

'Not from me.'

'Only one person can read it.'

'Who's that then?'

Liv looks out on Swans Island. 'That's for me to know.'

'How will they reach it?'

'They will.'

'You can tell me, I helped you *get* there.'

'It was something I had to do,' Liv says. 'Thanks for coming with me.'

'You planned it all along.' I knew she had, somehow.

'Yes, and I feel at peace with myself, now.' She strokes my hand with a swan's feather, and the wind whips over the grey lake beyond the window, and we both know we did something out there, and nothing will make us forget it. And though the war-bonnet project seems distant now, it feels like we earned those feathers in my bag, like the trip over the lake was our brave deed – that that was our *coup*, our successful stroke, to touch a part of ourselves, a part of ourselves, *together*.

'We'll be together, won't we? I mean, always be close, as sisters?'

'Always,' Liv says. And means it. And the waitress comes and asks us kindly to mind our elbows, and wipes up and takes our glasses, while the rain lashes the window outside, and mists the lake, and falls on the boulders on Swans Island, and the jar under the boulders on Swans Island, on the swans huddling against the wind, on the pumping station, on Evening Hill and the harbour beyond, where the currents run and the swans fly out over the sea . . .

'Still,' I'm saying, 'your message –'

'Get over it, will you?' Liv teases. 'Wouldn't you like to know?'

Actually, I would.

Later that day, while Liv takes a nap, I'm snooping around in her room, when I find her writing pad. No rough drafts of messages inside it. Nothing but notes for an essay on *Wuthering Heights,* headed 'Wuthering Heights Is Pants – discuss.' I'm about to put it away, when I notice the pad's been pressed on. Remembering her invisible ink phase, quills, codes, all that stuff, I find a soft pencil and shade softly over the top page, the page Liv pressed on last, perhaps when she wrote the message she put in the jar on the island –

Geronimo!

– a surprising white promise jumps out in Liv's handwriting against the dark grey pencil, and something about how hard she pressed, makes me think that she meant it:

To B or L, this Seventh Day of September 2001.
I, the Undersigned, Olivia Jane Bickle, Hereby Promise to Try to Do My Best For You For Ever and Ever, No Matter What. Maybe one day you'll come here and dig up this jar, and then you can tell me if I lived up to it, love

Mum

Chapter 23

'Bryony or Lewis?'

'You what?' Liv says, in the garden.

'For a name – how about Brandon or Lara?'

'Why "B"'s or "L"'s ?'

'Why not?'

Liv looks at me over her book. *You know something, don't you?* her eyes say.

I cover with, 'Sydney or Callum? Seriously. They're nice names. What about Ben, or Laura?'

'You're joking,' Liv says. 'Pass.'

'Benedict or Lauren then.'

'Mmm,' Liv goes. 'Maybe.'

'Beth or Lawrence?'

'No.'

'Brad or Letitia?'

Liv frowns and gets up with an effort, flopping into the hammock to enjoy what's left of the late summer sun, freakishly out this Saturday. For once the sound of the quad tearing around the field next door comes a close second to the whine of the circular saw from the barn, newly up this weekend, and chewing up firewood already.

'So peaceful Saturdays, isn't it?'

Liv ploughs on with *Jane Eyre*.

'Jane's a nice name.' Not. 'Lisa, Louisa, Leila. Bronwen, Bartholomew, Brett –'

'Shouldn't you be doing some work?' Liv rolls over, as much as she can, and her hair spills over the edge of the hammock. She's beautiful, my sister. The things she's done already, the arrangements she's made to go back to school, the clothes and the stuff she's collected, the classes she's going to, the folic acid she's taking, the things she's going without. 'You need to put some time in. Go over maths and German, so you know what to expect in Year Ten.'

'I know, but I'm not strong like you are.'

'Yes, you are.'

'No, I'm not.'

School work. I know she's right. I went back to school last Tuesday with a note saying: 'Sylvia has been excused games until further notice on the advice of Doctor Corvert', and a new denim pencil-case.

Later I'm up in the tree, thinking instead of studying, no text books opened, no coursework done, with the thick summer leaves closing me in and a blackbird twittering somewhere – when Luke comes by with his discman as usual, thinking he's so great, with what looks like a giftwrapped parcel under his arm.

He jumps up and down. Shouts for Liv through the hedge. 'Liv! I got something for you!'

Liv rolls out of the hammock and walks stiffly up to the hedge. 'Luke – what is it?'

'Got something for you.'

'What is it?' Liv says, wearily. 'Can't you push it through the hedge?'

'I could, but you wun't want me to,' boy wonder says, mysteriously.

Liv walks wearily round by the road. 'What is it then?' she says.

Luke brings out the giftwrapped parcel from behind his back.

A present for Liv. I'm curious.

'Got something for you,' he says.

Chapter 24

'Got something for you,' I'm telling Liv, even though it isn't ideal in the middle of the road, and Beddoes might walk by and catch us.

'What is it, Luke?' she goes.

So I planned to give it to her somewhere better, I never see her these days and, like Liv said sometime, you can't always have what you want. I went over it a million times. I could see she was out in the hammock through the coloured glass in the landing window, so I went and got it from under the bed, now or never, no turning back – it's only a casual present, right, what do I care who knows?

'It isn't anything much.' I'm wishing I never bought it now.

'Oh, Luke,' she says, 'you shouldn't have.'

'You undo the ribbon here. I meant to give it to you before, but somehow I never –'

'A Baby Mobile – Luke, that's so sweet.' She blushes when she looks up.

'S'on'y a thing I saw in Odyssey. I had to go there anyway.'

'I'm glad you did,' she goes. 'A mobile's perfect,' she goes. 'I haven't got one yet.' She likes it, I can tell.

'There's a matching cot-buffer, if you want it. I can get it, if you like.'

'What's a cot-buffer?' Liv says.

'It protects baby's head in his cot.'

'You know a lot about babies,' Liv says. 'He's not going to bang his head.'

'Or her head.'

'Or her head,' Liv goes.

'That's what I thought. Better go.'

But Liv calls me back. 'Luke –'

'What?'

'Thanks again.'

'No problem.'

Then she says, 'You know you work with Matt Kramer?'

'You could call it work,' I'm going.

'Well, he sent me this letter,' she goes, 'and I want to return everything. His parents are interfering, of course, and they open everything –'

'Want me to give it back, like the ring?'

'Would you, Luke?' she goes.

'No problem,' I'm going. I don't mind stuffing it to Kramer, any day of the week, so she slips this letter out of her book and hands it over –

'What is it?' she goes.

'This is my letter.'

'No, it's a letter from Matt.'

'It isn't, it's a letter from me.'

'Why would you write me a letter saying that our breaking up was a misunderstanding?'

'It doesn't say that.'

'Yes, it does.'

'Matt never wrote this,' I'm going. 'It's my letter. I wrote it, or Danny did anyway.'

'Danny?' Liv goes. 'What's he got to do with it?'

'I didn't want you to think I was stupid. I know what background is.'

'Background,' Liv says. 'Is this about "Loony Luke's Carwash"?'

'About the stories, yes.'

A stick rattles down from the top of the tree. Liv looks at the letter. The milkman stops at the junction. His empties clash as he brakes, looks left, and legs it up the road.

'I never thought you were stupid,' Liv says. 'Is that why it says, "I'm not as thick as I look"?'

'Danny left that in?'

'How about "oxymoron"?'

'Dunno.'

'I don't believe you wrote it,' Liv says. 'You're winding me up,' Liv says. 'Matt wrote this to impress me –'

'*I'm sorry if you misunderstood me the other day,*' I'm trying to remember what we wrote. '*I hope you can forget the things I said, so that we can start again. What's happened is a –* metaphor for stuff about cars –'

Liv sits down in the hedge. 'And I thought Matt made an effort.'

'The thing is Danny never posted it for ages, so maybe you got mixed up –'

'Big time,' Liv says, laughing, then crying.

'You all right?'

'He never *wanted* to get back together – yes, I'm all right,' she goes.

Bix comes down in a shower of sticks.

'Hope you got all that.' I forgot Ears was up the tree.

'Yes, thanks,' she goes. 'Very interesting.'

Bix takes the Baby Mobile out of its box and tinkles the bells around, and the dogs and the pigs and the cows walk and meet, walk and meet, and the little mirrors flash round. 'Loony Luke's got a heart. Who'd have thought it?' she goes.

Liv looks up. 'You know Matt –'

'Doesn't care, what's new?' Bix spins the mirrors around.

Kramer care, why would he? Kramer cares about himself. Long as he gets a new convertible the day he's eighteen, why would he think about Liv and the stuff she'll have to face? There's lots of reasons he *should* think about her, but none to dent Kramer's bodywork. I know more than Liv knows, how much Kramer cares.

And suddenly I'm thinking he should.

Those mirrors don't flash round one more time, chasing little spots of sunlight over Liv's face and clothes, before I decide Kramer's luck has run out, and I'm thinking I'll *make* him care.

Chapter 25

'What d'you want with that sugar?' Old man Kramer sights Luke across the forecourt with a packet of SuperSavers granulated. 'Sweet enough already, en't we?'

'Icing on it,' Luke says, holding the bag on his head.

Old man Kramer laughs. Natural comic, that boy. Pity he's back in school, but weekends are better than nothing. Regular talking point with the customers. Regular asset to the business. Sticks at things too. The old man eyes his son through the office window, feet up, head in *Autotrader*. If only Matt were more like Luke. Then business would go with a swing. 'You got customers, Luke?' he says. 'I could do with a hand in the workshop.'

Luke shuffles out from behind Matt's Escort. 'Making coffee,' he says, tapping the sugar to show that he's been interrupted in the process.

'Kettle don't live on the forecourt, in case you forgot.' Old man Kramer finds some change. 'Nip out and get us a *Mirror*.'

Luke heads for the newsagent, glad to be let off the hook, glad to let *himself* off the hook. What had seemed like a good idea last night took more bottle than he'd imagined. He'd felt like two people out there on the forecourt. The sugar spoon had hovered beside Matt's open filler cap. *Go on — he deserves it, no one's going to know. You're kidding, this'll rubbish his car, leave it out!*

Now the old man saw him messing about with the sugar. Still Luke takes the sugar for another walk, that afternoon.

'Yes-thank-you, Luke, we'll take two!' the old man bawls from the office.

'Two what?'

'Sugars in our tea. Mr Matcham's here. Get the kettle on, will you?'

Luke switches direction without missing a beat. Minutes later he appears in the office with a tray of tea and biscuits, two for the old man in his saucer, two for the oil-company representative, Mr Matcham, on the only unchipped plate at the garage, the sugar nicely presented in a Michelin Tyres ashtray.

'All at sixes and sevens, today?' The old man winks at Matcham. 'He forgot where we keep the kettle, din' you, Luke? Be washin' cars with tea next.'

'Or,' says Matcham thinly, 'putting out cigarettes in the sugar.' He takes two spoonfuls from the ashtray and eyes Luke over his cup.

'Hope it tastes all right,' Luke says. 'I brewed it in that old blue can. We like a bit of anti-freeze, don't we?'

The old man throws back his head. 'Matcham,' he says, 'you got one like this at home?'

'Can't say I have,' says Matcham. He drinks his tea in

fastidious little sips. 'Not having one, yourself?' he says to Luke.

'Customers,' Luke says, backing out and feeling nauseous. Outside the office, his heart thumps hard. Almost got caught that time. He'd covered well with the tea-making, but he'd got as far as opening Matt's petrol cap and *almost putting the sugar in*, before the old man had seen him. The Escort sits quietly at the side of the forecourt, its tank as yet unplugged by a giant wad of gunk created by a chemical reaction. Inside the shop Matt Kramer chats over his mobile with no idea how close his car just came to meltdown . . .

At four, the old man eyes Luke in the workshop. 'Not coming down with something, are you?'

Luke looks up. 'Sorry?'

'Not yourself today.'

'I think I might have a temperature,' Luke says, glad to use the excuse.

'You're white as a bag of sugar, yourself. I should get off home. You done enough for one day.'

Luke shies away from the old man's concern. If only he knew what he, Luke, had been trying to do all day, instead of being muddled or ill. He wrings out his shammy. Stacks his buckets. Loads a bumper bottle of Premier Turtle Wax carefully into his rucksack.

'Something on your mind?' the old man says.

'I can't do this any more,' Luke decides.

'Taking car-wax home?'

'The carwash,' Luke says. 'Sorry, but I've got too much homework.'

'Oh,' the old man says. 'Weekends, as well?'

'Sorry,' says Luke. 'My dad says I've got to do better this year.'

'In that case, you better stay home.'

'I c'n come back next year,' Luke says.

The old man digests the news slowly. 'Well, then, we're going to miss you.'

'I'll pick up the sign tomorrow, if that's all right.'

'You're good for business, Luke.' The old man peels a twenty-pound note off a roll in his pocket. 'Come back at Christmas, there's more where that came from.'

'Thanks, Mr Kramer.'

'Gordon.'

'Thanks, Mr Kramer.'

'You won't forget us, now, will you?'

'No chance.'

'Any time, Luke. I mean that.'

'Thanks, Mr Kramer.'

'Gordon.'

'G'bye.' Luke retreats in confusion and shoulders his rucksack. But Matt spots him leaving early and uses the forecourt microphone: 'Couch, where are you going? Couch! Pump four! Fill up the Escort, will you!'

Matt's voice crackles across the forecourt. Luke plods on, head down. Angrily, Matt leaves the shop and moves swiftly to block him. 'Not going anywhere, are we?'

'Fill up your own car, you dosser.' Luke ducks away, but Kramer won't leave it.

'Fill up the Escort or lose the pitch.'

'I lost it already.'

'Couch!'

'All right,' Luke says suddenly, turning.

'You can park it up for me after.' Kramer bowls him the keys.

The keys glint in the autumn sunshine, falling in a long arc through the golden air, gloriously, into his hands. Luke climbs into the Escort and brings it round to pump four. Kramer hasn't even noticed the petrol-cap's open.

Luke draws a petrol gun. Shielded from the office by an Astra and a Focus, he takes out a second gun. The first hose is green, for Premium Unleaded petrol. The second hose is black, for diesel.

The Escort takes unleaded, of course. Filling it up with diesel would send it straight to the workshop to have its engine and ignition system stripped down and cleaned, the workshop where the quad had sat for two weeks, having its engine cleaned.

Cool-Hand Luke closes his eyes and swaps guns from hand to hand, until his fingers no longer remember which gun is which. Fate's a funny thing. Gamble with people's emotions, someone's going to get hurt. Some things happen by chance. Then it's nobody's fault. Like what happened to Liv wasn't Matt's fault. Like it isn't his fault he's a loser. Like he doesn't deserve it. Like Luke's isn't the hand of fate.

Luke feels for the open filler cap.

Keeping his eyes closed, he stuffs a nozzle into the tank and holds in the trigger firmly. It isn't until he looks up to check that a perfectly rounded thirty quid's worth is charged to the business, that Cool-Hand Luke, the Hand of Fate, knows which fuel destiny has decided that Matt Kramer's Escort should have.

Chapter 26

Silence falls over the village. Except for the flapping of a sheet saying 'LIV – SWEET SIXTEEN' nothing moves very much, especially not the squashed hedgehog in the road, which hasn't moved for a while. Up on the Alfington roundabout, a torn and grey sheet still announces 'Naomi Griffiths Eighteen Today', the letters blotchy and vague now, and Naomi Griffiths herself, halfway to being nineteen.

A trail of posters of missing cats marks telegraph poles through the village. 'Tigger', the lost ginger tom on the Boys' Brigade door, looks yellowed and dog-eared now. Even the poster announcing the mysterious disappearance of Tiggy Bigglelowe is sodden inside its plastic wallet and has bled into the WI poster below announcing the Christmas Bazaar.

Rumours about Tiggy grow ridiculous.

Sightings from as far away as Sugden's Shop and Norden's Green vary almost as much as descriptions of his size and ferocity. 'Tiggy Bigglelowe, get out, it must be a panther,' old man Kramer remarks. 'He'll be the bleddy beast of Bodmin next – how big did you say he was?'

In the Paxmans' garden, Hodge the cat rises through the air and very nearly hooks a collared dove off the edge of the Paxmans' bird table. Mrs Chippy, watching from under the hedge, regards Hodge's mid-air twist with an unblinking stare as a single grey feather comes to rest between her ears. The feather trembles as Keith Hurst takes the White Cottage bend full-on in the Nova, his exhaust still hanging between the hedges as he roars back up on the Top Road, where he glimpses the new assistant up at the newsagent before braking in the last split-second before totalling into a lorry.

Opposite the newsagent, in Kitty's Kitchen across the road, Liv Bickle rewrites sections of a story over Kitty's cheap cola.

'Lashing out again, I see,' Paxman jokes, shouldering his way down the cramped little steps off the road and into the café. 'Just the one then?'

Liv's heart sinks. 'My third.'

'You're a sucker for punishment.'

'Someone has to drink it,' Liv says, the Paxman oldie tone and Weak Jokes Virus transferring itself depressingly easily. 'Anyway, it helps me to write.'

'Get you anything?' 'Kitty' enquires.

Paxman pays for the All-Day Breakfast at the counter and joins Liv, like she knew he would. 'What are you writing?' he asks, taking an unhealthy interest in the notepad she's protecting inside her arm.

'Nothing.'

'Taking a lot of trouble for nothing.' Paxman notes the rewrites and crossings-out.

'Why aren't you in school?' Liv asks Paxman.

'Frees this afternoon. You?'

'Studying at home, until after.'

Until *after* . . . Paxman digests the implication and tries to relate it to Liv's mysterious tummy, lost under the table in a velvet dress embroidered with mirrors. He watches Liv's hand cross the page. 'You jacked in the newsagent then.'

'Yes.'

'I expect you were glad to see the back of it.'

'Mmm,' Liv says, 'that's right.'

Paxman plays with the menu until his All-Day Breakfast arrives. Liv watches as he mixes tomato ketchup with his egg yolk, then folds the egg-white in half and downs it with his sausage.

'So what, you're a writer now?' Paxman asks through his sausage.

'Trying to be.'

'Put me in the story,' Paxman jokes. 'Liven it up a bit.'

Why would I want to do that? Liv considers the Walkman, the yellow puffa, the crop showing his shiny scalp. He used to look sad but unique. Now he looks like he hatched out of the same pod as everyone else.

'You used to look different,' Liv says. 'What happened to reading *World At War* at the bus stop?'

'Don't get it any more.'

'Any new birds on the bird table?'

'Dunno,' Paxman says warily, remembering to zip it, when near her.

'Scottish relatives?'

'They're fine.'

'Ghost stories? War films? Injuries?'

'I made striker for Alfington Football Club,' Paxman offers, tentatively. 'The strip's red, you should see it.'

'Loads of people play football,' Liv says. 'Not so many people know weird and interesting things.'

'I don't want to be weird,' Paxman says.

'You should get together with Bix. Two of a kind, you are.'

'She say that?' Paxman flushes.

'Not in so many words. She's into Native American culture and stuff like *Hiawatha* and thinking about things. She isn't afraid to be different.' Liv takes her time over a sentence. She looks up at last. 'Are you?'

'Fancy my Mars Bar?' Paxman says.

'Pass.'

'Got to go,' Paxman says, erupting out of his chair and knocking it over, then burping majestically as he straightens. 'Sorry, it –'

'– just came out.' Liv laughs. 'See you.'

Paxman crowds his way out of the door with a kind of tingle in his stomach, mixed up with egg and sausage, at the thought of being *two of a kind* with anyone, even, especially, with the provoking Bix up the tree.

Looking a wee bit pale as he leaves, Liv thinks. Unrecognizable without most of his hair. Michael Paxman,

Geekus Maximus, transformed into Puffa Man. At least now he knows when to go. Paxman learns the social graces at last, and when not to bore people to death. He might even quite like her sister.

She might even like him, once the idea grows legs. It saw Paxman off, anyway. Liv smiles to herself at the thought and buys herself another 'Coke' on the strength of it, the first and only time in her life she managed to shut Paxman up.

'Come down out of that tree.'

Bix peers down between her legs to see Michael Paxman in that hideous yellow jacket looking determinedly up at her. 'Why should I?'

'Because it's weird.'

'And you're not?'

'Come down,' Paxman insists. 'No one else sits up a tree. Be like everyone else.'

'Look like you, you mean?'

'What's that supposed to mean?'

'Ditch the puffa, it's hideous. I liked you the way you were.'

'That's why you called me Geekus Maximus.'

'You said it went double for me,' Bix reminds him. 'Why don't you just be yourself?'

'Why don't you stop pretending to be ill?' Fighting talk from Paxman.

'I am ill, what d'you think, I'm pretending?'

'But you could come back to school.'

'I *am* back at school.'

'Full-time, like everyone else.'

No one has talked this directly to Bix in a long time. Sounds like he *wants* her to come back to school. Like not much is actually preventing her.

'Coming down then?'

'What's it to you?'

'Pick 'n' Mix?' He rattles a bag. 'Got a book about birds at home.'

'So?'

'*A History of the American Eagle.* The cultural importance of eagle feathers to Native American peoples,' Paxman says, carelessly.

Tempting, but no. A million cutting remarks occur to Bix. What is she, a kid, to be lured down with sweets and a bird book? But today she doesn't feel cutting. She feels fourteen, where he's sixteen. And Paxman, he isn't bad-looking. 'Swans, as well?'

'If you like. Plus I've got pictures of Luke.'

'Pictures of Luke?'

'Running away from Mrs Turpitz. Innit took 'em – classic stuff, want to see?' Silence while a breeze ruffles the tree. 'Coming down then?'

'Flattered you care.'

'I'm flattered you should come down.'

'Quaint thing to say.'

'Quaint,' says Mike. 'That's me.'

After a long moment in which Michael Paxman downs shrimps and bootlaces ostentatiously in front of her, strange and sylvan Sylvie Bickle – aka Bix, The Wild One, Gorilla Girl – slides down the tree to join him.

Back at Kitty's Kitchen the extractor fan hums over the crackle of hot fat and explosive cackles of laughter, as the vinegar is handed between a newly arrived gaggle of pensioners anxious to get their dentures around the Cod 'n' Chips Lunchtime Special. Liv frowns. Can't help but hear. *Must they talk so loud?*

'Bill's under Doctor Renfrew –'

'Doctor Benbow?'

'RENFREW. He said, he's going to Swindon –'

'Sweden?'

'SWINDON, to see his daughter –'

Twenty minutes after Paxman's departure, Liv clicks off her biro and folds away her writing pad. Writing, whether you feel like it or not, is hard work. Writing while chomping pensioners around you size up their lemon meringue pie before they've necked their chips, isn't exactly inspirational.

And the story? A little thin, perhaps. She could start again. Put in all the things that she couldn't see *needed* to go in, the first time round. Plenty of time to write it now. Let the story come out the way it wants to . . .

After a while the pen wanders, and she finds herself writing a letter, a reply to that letter of Loony Luke's that had shown her her heart in such a strange way, by showing her what she *hadn't* wanted, when it came to it, a make-up with Matthew Kramer . . .

Dear Luke, You sent me a letter once, so I thought I'd write one back. I suppose I might have known that Matt didn't write the letter. I wanted to believe that he had, so I blocked out everything else. I don't think people who don't know about writing are stupid. I haven't made you stupid in my story, but you see, it isn't you. What writers do, is spin a whole story from a sign, a name, a tiny idea or a dog. All the characters in the story that comes with this letter are made up, except for Tiggy Bigglelowe and a character made up from your name and the bits of the carwash I've seen. I borrowed a few other things about you, if I'm honest. Hope we're still friends. Liv.

That evening Paxman roots in the bin and retrieves the *Wild Guide to British Birds*. Under 'Swans' he finds:

'Mute Swan. *Cygnus olor*. Familiar bird of lakes and slow-moving rivers. Pairs nest singly. 5–8 eggs hatch after 36 days. Young swim soon after hatching and may ride on their parents' backs.'

Get off and walk, Paxman thinks, noting the familiar picture of a white swan with an orange beak. The other swans listed, Bewick's Swan, *Cygnus columbianus* (swan-that-is-dove-like) and the Whooper Swan, *Cygnus cygnus* (Swan-swan) look nothing like the swans at Lakey Park. Not that he and Bix had talked about swans, or even about American eagles . . .

Instead, they'd spent the afternoon and early evening talking about a million and one things they had in common. He'd even put on his football kit for her, and she hadn't laughed, and he hadn't been embarrassed, and it had seemed completely natural to show her, and she'd said she'd come and see him play, sometime. The thought of playing in front of her had shot into his heart like a bolt. She'd told him things she'd never told anyone before. She told him she'd made a replica of Cochise's war-bonnet out of swans' feathers. She hadn't told anyone that, though Luke and Danny had seen her in it, and Danny had run in, scared. 'Danny's all right,' Paxman had laughed. 'I know he is,' she'd agreed. They actually had a lot in common. 'We actually have a lot in common,' she'd actually said that. 'Haven't we, Mike?' she'd said. She did actually say 'actually' a lot. Got him doing it now.

Somehow the time had flown by, and his mother was inviting her to stay for an evening meal. 'Would Sylvia like to stay for tea?'

'It's Sylvie – and she's going now.'

'I'm sure we can tempt her with smoked haddock –'

'Thanks anyway, Mrs Paxman,' Sylvie had declined.

But she'd said she'd come back, tomorrow . . .

Paxman looks in the mirror and sees himself with a girl-friend. How different does that make him look? He strikes a few poses – the hair's growing back. Should he grow back the bowl or not? Sylvie had said she liked him the way he was. But the bowl is a haircut too far. Probably licked up with gel would be good, maybe in a point down the middle? Then again, dare to be different – start a fashion to be yourself. Go with the bowl, why not?

Sylvie. Sylvia. Gross name, but one he's determined to like. Sylvias will never be same for the rest of his life. Paxman looks it up in *One Thousand Best Baby Names*, a book which has stood on his shelves for so long, no one knows where it came from.

Paxman leafs through 'S – Girl'. 'Sarah – Serena – Shirley.' Here it is: 'Sylvia – Sylvana – (*Latin*) 'of the trees or woods.'

'Of the trees', of course. Sylvie's light-blonde hair up the tree, the sun flashing through it as she looks down and speaks, her slim, white legs on the branches . . .

Paxman goes to bed and dreams that a tree shows him ball skills, and is, in fact, Michael Owen. Later that night, a flash of yellow in the moonlight wakes him up.

Whose is that horrible yellow puffa over the chair?

Hideous thing. Paxman gets up and moves it. It had never felt like his. It felt like someone else's skin, Loony Luke's, maybe . . . Paxman tosses and turns. Just its presence in the room annoys him, like something *out of place* . . . What time is it? Twelve-ten? What can he do to get to sleep?

At twelve minutes past twelve precisely, a figure pads down the hall. Passing prints of pheasants in Scots' glens, nooks filled with knick-knacks and sprays of dried Honesty, photos of himself at primary school, framed piano grades – even china plates showing children simpering over puppies – Michael knows that they're a part of himself, as much as his teeth or his nails. This is the house he grew up in. Now his job is find the rest of himself, not to fit in with everyone else. Be true to yourself. Reject the rest. You're not Luke Couch. You've been framed.

At fourteen minutes past twelve exactly, as his old

parents snore over the deep-carpeted, creaking hallway, Michael David Paxman, reaching the hall stand, daring to be himself, no matter how sad, hangs up his puffa for good.

Chapter 27

So Liv gets me this book from the library called *Build Your Own Business?* Turns out I've been doing all the right things without knowing it. No wonder Loony Luke's Carwash took off. I checked them off on the Checklist To Success. So the Seventeen Essential Qualities for Building A Successful Business are:

1. **Ambition** – yes.
2. **Persistence** – yes.
3. **Endurance** – yes, same thing.
4. **Obduracy** – what?
5. **Understanding** – how to make money?
6. **Empathy** – I looked it up, it means 'power of losing one's sense of identity in contemplation of a work of art, person, or object.' – What?
7. **Articulation** – or being able to say, 'Want your car washed?'
8. **Confidence** – overload.
9. **Decisiveness** – decided I don't need this list.
10. **Humour** – no worries.

11. **Persuasion** – I cleana your car, or I wreck it, OK?
12. **Intuition** – about a carwash??
13. **Temperance** – thought it meant not getting drunk on the job, turns out it means 'moderation'.
14. **Patience** – not.
15. **Style** – big time.
16. **Service** – five star.
17. **Humility** – sorry?
18. **The End.**

Not counting the ones I don't understand, fourteen out of fifteen, check it out. The next bit's headed *Qualities to Add Steeliness*, whatever Steeliness is. Some of the other chapters are headed *Marketing Your Enterprise*, *Maintaining Progress* and *Powering Your Way To Success*.

I think I did enough powering. I'm sticking with my customer-base now. Loyal customers are the Foundation of Any Enterprise, it says here. Under 'Competition' it says, 'List the main competitors in your immediate catchment area'. There was a time, not so long ago, when I thought I might have to do that, until Mental Mike and Crazy Chris turned out to be Paxman's wind-up.

Now I packed in the garage till next year, or maybe for ever, I'm just washing cars round the village these days. I'm out there the other morning, hosing off Mrs Oliff's Corsa, sun shining, not thinking about anything in particular, wondering what gives with Gorilla Girl since she stopped sitting up the tree – when a cat wanders over the road, so I give it a dab with the hose.

'Lovely morning,' Mr Paxman says, coming round the corner with a letter.

'I'll post that for you, if you like,' I'm going. 'Give the old legs a rest.'

'I like to walk,' he goes, 'but thank you anyway, Luke.'

'Is that Hodge still eating your birds?'

'He doesn't come over very often,' he says. 'Thanks for fixing it.'

'I just fixed another,' I'm going. 'A tabby with one white foot?'

'Oh,' he goes, 'Rosie Startup's Molly.'

'No,' I go, 'Mrs Chippy.'

'It can't be Mrs Chippy,' Mr Paxman goes. 'Mrs Oliff's cat went missing.'

'That's why it's living at Startups'.'

'How do you know?'

'Seen it,' I go.

'But how on earth can the same cat –'

'I think we got a double-agent.'

'Better let it stay that way.' Old-man Paxman winks.

I'm taking my time with the Corsa. Might as well give Mrs Oliff a wicked-looking car if she only owns half a cat. I like to do a good job. Confidence in Job Well Done is on the list of Qualities To Add Steeliness, so I'm probably well Steeled already. As Innit said the other day, 'You give it the hundred per cent, bound to count for summink, innit?'

'Not with your mum,' I go. 'She gave me stick when I called.'

'Good laugh, though, wannit?' he goes. 'Paxman put me

up to it, after you warned him off the carwash, that time.'

'Crazy Chris, as if.'

'My mum never meant anything.'

'What about the pictures?'

'What pictures?' he goes.

'There's photos going around.'

'I never took any photos. My mum, innit?' Innit goes. 'Obvious I never tookum.'

'Thanks a lot for setting me up, mate.'

'Joke, innit?'

Payback, innit? I'll tell him, when the photos reach Mrs Turpitz, and she goes purple from the neck up, and probably grounds Innit for ever. What are you whining about? I'll be able to say. Justice, innit? What goes around, comes around, dunnit?

I'm hosing below the splash-line, when Mrs Oliff sticks her head out of the window. 'Lemon barley water, Luke?'

She balances a glass of this cloudy muck on the window-ledge. I tried it once. Tastes like old people's wardrobes smell. Biggest treat in the world.

'Cheers, Mrs Oliff.'

Soon as her head goes in, it's a swift move to the flower-bed. Remember to put the glass back, and look as if you enjoyed it. But now she leans out with the jug. 'That was quick – like a top-up, Luke?'

I give her a burp. 'No room.'

'Car looks nice.'

'Dry polish today.'

'Is that better?'

'Takes a bit longer, but yeah.'

'Sure I can't give you more lemon barley water?'

'You can if you want me to burst.'

'I know what *you'd* like,' she says, going in to ferret out some mothball-smelling biscuits or something.

So it's a swift finish with some new car wax today, to give the Corsa a treat – Triplewax, The Original Easy Shine Auto Wax, A Brilliant Shine Without Effort.

So I'm reading the back of the bottle as I'm hosing, wondering why the directions sound rude in Dutch – *Lost modder en vuil snel op.* (Your mother smells, or, Quickly penetrates dirt and grime.) *Sterk schuimend, waardoor scherpe deeltjes worden opgenomen.* (The stork has herpes, the warden had an operation, or, Added foam booster lifts damaging particles.) *Brengt glans op chroom en carrosserie.* (Boiled glands and carrots, or, Brings up chrome and bodywork) – when someone goes by in the road.

As soon as I spot the yellow puffa through the hedge, I let him have it with the hose. *Paxman, I owe you, take that!* I get him right between the shoulder-blades with a power-blast by jamming the hose with my thumb and cranking up the supply from the tap to hit him even harder. *Eat that, Paxman, you loser, tables turned now, or what!*

The power-jet nails him in the back and almost knocks him over. I keep it trained on his head as he tries to turn round. He tries again, but I pile on the grief till he's forced to turn back, his legs buckling as I give him the full power-blast in the back of the knees. And he's trying to turn again, asking for it this time, when suddenly *Ben Dent* jumps out of

234

Paxman's puffa and stands screaming in the middle of the road.

'I'll tell my dad you did this, Couch, *you'll never wash cars up The White Hart again!*' Dent legs it, blubbering and hollering.

Nice one, Luke. And I'm remembering now that Ben Dent's dad part owns The White Hart with Jim Bowyer, so I probably blew that out now, along with the Kramer concession. It's bad news for the carwash. Could be the end of the business, just when I was Powering My Way to Success and Adding Steeliness.

Truth is, I'm fed up of it, anyhow. But I didn't think it would end like this. Things never turn out like you think.

I know I shouldn't've tried to hose him down in the road, even though he hosed *me*. I know I shouldn't chuck his stuff in the hedge. I know I shouldn't wind him up for being Geekus Maximus, then for *not* being Geekus Maximus. I know I should've let him fit in, that some people think I'm a prat, that I *am* a prat, sometimes.

But I still don't have a clue why Paxman gave Ben Dent his jacket.

Chapter 28

Confessions, Seven. I'm not Bix any more, I'm Sylvie. I quite like the name Sylvie, now. Mike says he likes it a lot. He says it means 'of the trees', but I'm not of the tree any more.

Sylvie 4 Mike – I even saw it written on the back of a seat on the school bus! But I do actually like Mike a lot. We've been seeing each other every day, actually since I came down out of the tree, almost tree, sorry three, weeks ago, now. I don't even think about the tree any more. There's too much happening on the ground.

Mike and I get on really well. We do actually have a lot in common. The other day a funny thing happened, and we had to make a joint decision, and I liked Mike even more. We were spending the day in town, me and Mike, when we caught the five-twenty bus home –

I should probably start from the beginning.

Me and Mike are on our way home from town after the cinema, shopping, etc. – Mike even waited in the sad boyfriends queue while I tried things on in Top Girl – when we're on the five-twenty bus home, when this dog hops on at St Mullion.

'The bus-driver stopped for it – look!' I'm saying to Mike. 'That dog got on by itself.'

'Must have been shopping,' Mike jokes. He's got a really dry sense of humour.

The dog sits down by the driver. The driver gives it a Choco-Dog pet-treat out of a bag, like he's expecting it or something, and then we pull away and the dog settles down by the luggage rack. It's when the dog looks round that there's something about its face –

'It's a German shepherd too.' Those paws. The blotchy bit on his side and the feathery tail with the bit missing. The dog thumps its tail when I catch its eye. It's becoming really obvious that it has to be – 'Tiggy Bigglelowe!'

'Never,' Mike says.

'Why not, he has to be somewhere – it is, look, his paws are the same.'

The German shepherd crosses its paws as though it knows we're talking about it.

'It's similar,' Mike says. 'But Tiggy would have had your hand off by now.'

'Maybe he's changed.'

'You think?'

'It is Tiggy Bigglelowe – Tiggy!' The dog thumps its tail even more. 'I'm going up to ask the driver.'

'Sylvie –'

'Back in a minute.'

'Excuse me,' I'm asking the driver, more certain than ever that it's Tiggy, now I can see him up close, 'but d'you often stop for this dog, here?'

'Every day,' the driver nods. 'A regular, ain't you, Rover?'

'Every day? Where does he go?'

'The bus depot. He comes back with me on the five-twenty bus, and we have a bit of something in the office, don't we?'

'Rover' wags 'yes' at the driver and sneezes three times.

I'm determined to get to the bottom of this. 'So he goes with you to the depot – how does he get to St Mullion?'

'Nine o'clock bus every morning,' the bus driver says.

'What does he do in St Mullion all day?'

'Goes to the butcher's. Warrens give him sausages. Regular as clockwork. Even the postie knows him.'

'And he comes back with you on this bus, and sleeps at the bus depot.'

'Guards it,' the driver says. 'He's obviously trained as a guard dog – know him, do you?'

'Yes,' I'm telling the driver, 'I do. His name's Tiggy Bigglelowe. He's been missing for weeks.'

'No collar,' the driver says. 'Not missing from some-where near here?'

'Middlehill,' I'm trying to tell him, while Tiggy Biggle-lowe licks my hand. 'He must enjoy travelling by bus. He used to be really savage.'

'Mild as milk, now, en't you?' the driver says.

'Rover' bangs his tail on the floor.

'Wants to speak, but he ain't got no woof, 'ave you?' The driver ruffles his head.

Mike comes up and joins in. 'Didn't you wonder where he came from?'

The driver shrugs. 'Seemed to know where he was going. Loves his Cumberland sausages. But then, if it's like you say . . .'

'It's Tiggy,' I'm saying to Mike. 'I think we should take him home.'

Mike frowns. 'Do we have to?'

'I can actually hear my stereo since he disappeared, but then –'

'Suppose we never saw him?' Mike says.

'Someone else is bound to.'

'He seems to like catching the bus,' Mike says.

'Yes, but Mrs Bigglelowe –'

'He's slimmer, and not so vicious – why not leave him, if he's happy? You're right,' Mike sighs. 'I'm just thinking how peaceful it's been. I suppose we should take him home.'

So the secret life of Tiggy Bigglelowe came to an end, at last. He'd got himself a job at the bus depot as a guard dog, with wages of food and a bed. He'd got himself a regular run to the butcher's, to get sausages. He enjoyed travelling and had seen a bit of the world. All in all, as Mike says, Tiggy Bigglelowe had done quite well for himself. Not quite as well as Mrs Chippy, aka Molly, the tabby cat, whose double life had been exposed last week in a ding-dong between the Startups and Mrs Oliff. Luke had come down on Mrs Oliff's side, but the Startups had since forgiven him, when he went out and got them a kitten.

He hadn't been eating double rations every day, like Mrs

Chippy, but the secret life of Tiggy Bigglelowe had been going on for weeks, and now it was about to end – like peace and quiet round the village.

Mike has his finger on the Bigglelowes' doorbell, when he turns to look at me. 'Shall we?'

Bringing home the village foghorn, what are we, mad? 'Go on then.'

Mike's eyes smile. There's a moment before we ring the bell. Tiggy jumps up and joins in the kiss, in his last few minutes as 'Rover'. Soon he'll be tied to a peg in the lawn, savaging shadows and barking.

'Ready?' Mike rings the bell on the end of peace and quiet. Mrs Bigglelowe grows larger through the frosted glass door, and when she opens it, she isn't even grateful. 'My darling, what have they *done* to you?'

'Made him a lot slimmer?' Mike hands 'Rover' over.

'Oh, he's come back to me, after all.' Prodigal doggie licks Mrs Bigglelowe's face with his disgusting tongue. 'Tiggy-wiggy, where 'ave you *been*?'

'Eating sausages in St Mullion,' Mike says.

'What d'you mean, sausages?' Mrs Bigglelowe says, suspiciously.

'Cumberland sausages, apparently.'

''Aven't got his collar, 'ave you?' She looks at us like we're hiding it. 'Mind you shut the gate on the way out, I can't be chasing him up the road,' says Mrs Bigglelowe, the witch.

Next day, poor old Tiggy's pegged out on the lawn, like he never left it. Mike walks past him. 'Listen – no bark!'

'You're right! The bus driver said he "ain't got no woof"!'

And the funny thing is, he hasn't. Maybe Tiggy Bigglelowe left his bark in St Mullion, or barked himself hoarse guarding the bus depot every night, which was actually what he was trained to do in the first place. Maybe he traded his woof for a pound of Cumberland sausages, but he didn't come home with it.

Now when we pass him, he sneezes or yawns. He doesn't even strain on his tether. Maybe the travelling cured him. Maybe he saw enough of the world, and he likes Middlehill as well as anywhere. Maybe he *can* bark, but doesn't, who knows? But over the village silence reigns, except for the quad on a weekend, and the holiday-park disco on Fridays. Even Keith Hurst went quiet, these days. Seems too good to be true.

Two things, before I go. The tree went electric on the twenty-eighth of October, after lightning brought down the power lines, and the power lines brought down some branches. There isn't a lot left of it now, after South West Power came out with a chain-saw to make it 'safe', i.e. cut most of it down. And I'm not saying anything *else* about things I see up the tree, but if you're still wondering whether someone deliberately released Tiggy Bigglelowe months ago to shut him up, I'm not giving away a lot when I'm pointing out what *Mister* Bigglelowe says up the pub.

'Enough's enough,' he says, up the pub. 'I always say, I said at the time, enough is enough is enough.'

Now I can lie in any time I want. I can study, hear my

stereo, everything's fine. Mike comes over and makes me laugh, and I don't get so tired any more, or nervous, and I don't mind school any more, and I wonder – when I see the bits of the tree that are left – why I spent so long looking down, when I could've been looking up.

Liv's well, and ready to pop. Sometimes I think about Swans Island, and about the promise she left there in the jar. I try to imagine Brandon or Luke, or Betty or Barnaby or Lucy or Lois going to see it; taking a boat with their mates; battling over the lake; digging up that old, rusty jar, and reading the message inside it. *I, the Undersigned, Promise to Try to Do My Best for You for Ever and Ever, No Matter What . . . Maybe one day you'll come here and dig up this jar, and then you can tell me if I lived up to it . . .*

I try to see him or her, a blurry future figure, making a promise of their own, that day.

But perhaps Lakey Park will be history then, the Café rusting, the lake dry, the swans all flown away.

But until then, I can think about it. I know Liv does, sometimes.

Chapter 29

Might as well close Accounts now. That's it for the 'Loony Luke's Carwash' Profit and Loss book. Danny found it the other day and used it to clean out the chickens.

I could of killed him when I found it. 'You did *what?*'

'I scraped out the henhouse with it. You left it lying around.'

'In the barn, you mean.'

'I thought it was old,' Danny goes. 'My glasses misted up. I couldn't *see* it, could I?'

'That's right, milk the glasses.'

'You milk cows, not glasses, stupid.'

'All right, blinkers, I will.'

Give him credit, he's a lot better to live with. He used to get so frustrated. Now he's not so clumsy, plus he's King of the Quad. Danny makes the Firestarter do things it wasn't designed for, Dad says. Let's hope he never rolls it.

I could of killed him when he balanced the books by covering them with poo and binning them. But I suppose the books balance up, now Danny closed accounts on the Carwash and everything else last summer, and everyone got what they wanted, or even what they didn't want. On the Loss side, Kramer's a crap father. On the Gain side, he lost his car.

Turns out I never put in the wrong petrol after all, and Kramer tools around until Christmas before he meets Keith Hurst head-on on Tunbrook Bends opposite the sugar factory.

Kramer v. Hurst on black ice, totalled both their motors, lucky not to top themselves. Police said it would've been worse if the Nova hadn't concertina-ed and taken the shock. Notorious bend for accidents, yet Hurst was photographed doing eighty along the Top Road moments before. You were fortunate not to have left the road, or topped-out in the pig farm below, the policeman who interviewed him goes. Wouldn't have been so clever, would it, son? No, Hurst goes, it wouldn't. Lucky, aren't you, the policeman goes, doing him for dangerous driving.

Hurst had a grudge against Kramer for two-timing his sister, so it was what Danny'd call ironic that they went and ran into each other. I was glad for old man Kramer that no one got hurt, not sorry that Matt the love-rat got what was coming to him. 'He lost his car after all, big laughs all round,' I'm going to Dan.

'What d'you mean, after all?'

'Kramer escapes the Hand of Fate, then meets Hitman Hurst and gets it in the neck, anyway.'

Danny goes, 'What Hand of Fate?'

So Kramer gets what's coming to him. He even left school for a dead-end job. He has to pay Liv every month.

The old man told him get out and earn it. He sends Liv things for the baby, his mum does anyway. That's about it for pasty-factory boy. Might even make company director, in time. That's if he sweeps enough floors.

Liv had her baby at Christmas. She called him Kieran Mark. She was going to call him Byron Mark, Lydia if it was a girl, but Bix went and talked her out of it – good job, I went and told her.

'Byron?' I'm asking Liv.

'What do you know?'

'Nothing, I'm ignorant, me.'

'As if,' she goes, and smiles.

Liv's in the Lower Sixth now, doing A Level English literature, maths, French. They said she couldn't mix English and maths, but Liv just goes, Why not? and does it anyway. Pigeonholes are bad, she says. You shouldn't limit yourself.

Me, I'm not pigeonholed either. Danny and me branched out.

Babysitting Two-fifty An Hour
Loony Luke & Dumb Danny
Children Guaranteed Amused

Harder than doing the Carwash, but at least there's telly and pizza, and Dan does the nappy-changes. Joint business venture. Two for the price of one. I like babies a lot. I could go into child-care, Mum says. May even be a nurse, why not? I like being Uncle Luke.

Liv's going to give me a lift to school every day when she

passes her driving test. When Liv drives to school in the car with her mum, they give me a lift now, sometimes. When Bix misses the bus, she comes with us. Old Kieran Mark, he comes too. She leaves him in the crèche in the Sports Centre. Crèche is a French word like *chamois*. I looked it up in the dictionary. It means 'public day nursery for infants whose mothers are at work'. Why not just say nursery? Or goat-shaped antelope skin for cleaning cars?

Liv said writing stories got her through. She gave me a story to read, but I never got round to reading it yet. Danny read it and said it's a laugh. I never get time to read, these days.

I'm not doing the Carwash this year.

Once I blew out The White Hart on Sundays by hosing Ben Dent in mistake for Paxman, because Paxman gave Ben Dent his puffa because he, Paxman, didn't like it any more and Ben Dent thought Paxman was cool – how was I to know anyone would ever think Paxman was cool – it was never going to be worth my while.

Now I do dog-walking after school. Sometimes I take Tiggy Bigglelowe out in a muzzle. That would be Tiggy Bigglelowe in the muzzle, not me. Mrs Bigglelowe says he's not vicious, it's just that he bit a hole in someone's trousers out of frustration with losing his bark, and not being able to travel by bus to pick up his Cumberland sausages.

But, as Innit said the other day, 'When you keep a guard dog, it's bound to happen, innit?'